THE
SILVER
SPOON

BY
CARL 'A OTTO

Illustrations on front cover and page i by the author

ISBN: 1-58597-385-8

Library of Congress Control Number: 2006925369

4500 College Boulevard
Overland Park, KS 66211
888-888-7696
www.leatherspublishing.com

Dedication

This book is dedicated to the memory of my mother, Myrtle Mae Watson Otto. She had a vivid imagination and was an excellent storyteller. I have had numerous individuals tell me, "You sound like your mother."

So, Mom, "Here's to you. I hope your predictions about heaven are true, and that you are spinning tales to all your old hillbilly relatives and friends. I know I have inherited your imagination. For that I am truly thankful."

Foreword

This is a story about a young man who, as the old saying goes, was born with a silver spoon in his mouth and who has known nothing but wealth his entire life. At age 32 he is involved in a situation in which he begins to understand that wealth is not necessarily the main key to happiness. He meets a young man who is about his age; the young man has a beautiful wife, two great kids and a fulfilling job. Dalton begins to realize he is living the shallow life of a spoiled playboy. He decides to make a change.

Is it possible for a man in his 30s, who has never wanted for anything in his life; who has always lived in a mansion and has never experienced a day of labor, who has had servants wait on him, clean up after him and see to his every need, and whose only concern is self-gratification, to actually change his lifestyle? We shall see.

About the Author

Carl A. Otto is a self-described "old fart alley rat." He was past the age of 80 when he finished this, his fourth book; and, he has at least three more on the drawing board. He was born in Pierce, Nebraska, during the roaring 20s; he has survived the Great Depression and combat service during World War II, and although he was a high school drop-out, he retired from a career as an educator that featured moving up through the ranks as a teacher and athletic coach, high school and elementary principal and, finally, a superintendent of schools his last 15 years before retirement.

He lives alone on a farm in southeast Kansas where his late wife of nearly 54 years was born and raised. He is the father of two sons, one of whom is a school administrator; the other is a Kansas state legislator, after retiring from a career as a educator.

When not involved in writing, he spends as much time as possible with his sons and daughters-in-law, his six granddaughters, four grandsons, his three grandsons-in-law and his four great-grandchildren. He is also a Red Coat hospital volunteer.

Table of Contents

The Silver Spoon

FOR AS LONG as Dalton James Heinkle, Jr. can re-member, he has had the proverbial silver spoon in his mouth. He has no memory of ever wanting something he did not get — until now. He is 32 years old, and suddenly he is beginning to realize he is not a happy person. He begins to see himself for what he really is when he attends the annual company picnic. This pic-nic is an event that has been taking place every fourth of July, in the company park, for as long as Dalton can remember. He attended the event with his parents when he was a child, but by the time of his 13th birthday, he had reached a point in his rich brat days where he re-fused to go. He felt he was so much better than the children of the company hard-hats that he should not waste his time with what he considered an ignorant, smelly bunch.

Dalton's father always hosted the event, and he did spend quite a sum of money on having a catering ser-vice supply the food. Behind his back, the workers

1

called him the "Great White Father." Dalton James Heinkle, Sr. used the occasion to recognize outstanding achievements by individuals, accomplishments of certain divisional work, and for the awarding special bonuses. Dalton assumed his father to be a good boss; however, it was doubtful there was a single worker on the payroll who did not feel the Great White Father could easily provide much larger and many more bonuses. The truth of the matter was, they were right.

The Heinkles are like so many wealthy families. They have so many worldly things, they long ago began to think they are better than others. Mr. Heinkle hosts these picnics to "boost morale," and in so doing, boost production. It works, but employees are not fooled. The workers assume the attitude of, "What the hell; it's here, we might just as well enjoy the day."

This year, Dalton's dad told him, "Son, one of these days you are going to wake up and find that you are responsible for this company. I am not getting any younger. I now have reasonably good health, but that could change. You need to get more involved."

"Oh, Dad, why don't you turn the operation of the company over to Fredrick?"

"Because Fredrick is my son-in-law, and you are my son. And besides, Fredrick already has a career."

Mr. Heinkle went on to say, "You are now 32 years old, and all you seem to be interested in is driving expensive automobiles and chasing after shallow women."

Dalton could not debate that issue.

His father continued, "I am not saying you have to attend, but I am asking you to simply be by my side during the ceremonies at the picnic this year."

Dalton looked into his father's face for a moment. He could see a tear in his eye.

"Sure I will, Dad. I promise I will be there. In fact, I will be there all day, and I will mingle with the employees."

On the day of the event, Dalton awoke at his usual time, around 10 a.m. He stretched a bit and got up to go to the bathroom.

Suddenly it hit him, "Oh, hell, this is the fourth of July. I promised Dad I would go to that damned picnic."

He dressed and headed straight for the park. When he arrived, his dad was in his usual position, sitting on a lounge chair under the shelter house. Dalton hurried straight toward him. When the elder Heinkle saw his son coming, he stood up and started toward him.

"Oh, great, Son, you did decide to come after all."

Dalton told him he was sorry for being late.

His father said, "It's okay, the main thing is, you came."

Dalton went to the food table to get myself a cup

of coffee and a sweet roll. As he was pouring his coffee, a fellow about his age walked up to fill his cup. As he did, he extended his right hand.

"Hi, you must be new with the company, I don't believe we have met. My name is George."

It was an awkward moment for Dalton. He had been working at his father's company, if you could call what he did working, since he graduated from college.

Dalton answered, "No, I guess we have not met."

He extended his hand and George gripped it, as he flashed a firm warm, friendly smile.

Dalton continued, "My name is Dalton."

George answered, "Dalton! How about that, you have the same name as the Great White Father."

"The Great White Father? Who is that?"

"That's the old man — Old Man Heinkle."

Dalton did not know what to say or do, but after an embarrassing pause, he said, "I'm afraid I am Dalton Heinkle, Jr. The Great White Father is my dad."

He thought George was going to drop his coffee, as he just stood speechless.

Dalton said, "Don't think anything of it, George. It's understandable you would not know me. I rarely, if ever, get around the workers."

He continued, "Actually, I knew who the Great White Father was; I was pulling your leg."

He lied.

About the time George started to tell Dalton he was sorry, two small children ran up to him, calling him Daddy. Not far behind the two children was a very pretty young woman.

George said, "Dalton — I mean Mr. Heinkle — this is my family."

Dalton answered, "I am not Mr. Heinkle. That is Mr. Heinkle over under the shelter house; I am Dalton."

George's wife said, "Oh, I'm sorry. Did I interrupt something?"

"No, you didn't interrupt a thing."

They exchanged the usual small talk, and Dalton went back to his father.

He was thinking, *"I am about his age, with absolutely nothing except that damn tasteless silver spoon in my mouth, along with the prospects of becoming the owner of the family company."*

He returned to his dad and sat down in a chair beside him.

"Dad, I just met a fellow about my age."

Before he could say more, his father said, "Yes, Son, I saw you talking to George Flynn. He is one of our better foremen."

Dalton continued, "Yes, and do you know what? He had no idea who I was. But as we talked, I realized it was no fault of his. Hell, I doubt there are five workers here today who would recognize me."

"Well, Son, you don't spend much time at the plant, and when you are there, it is only in the offices."

He thought, *"Dad is right. I really do not know a thing about this company, except that I get a regular transfer to my checking account that I do not really earn."*

He looked around at the people as they stood in small groups. There were kids all over the place. Everyone seemed to be having a good time. Periodically, some individual would walk up to Dalton's father and exchange a few words.

Dalton soon began to realize that he did not recognize any of the people. His father seemed to know all of them, at least the ones who came to him for a short visit. He also began to realize that none of the top executives in the company were present. The truth of the matter, Dalton spent so little time, even in headquarters, that he was not sure he would recognize any of the central office staff members, even if they were present.

The Noble Idea

DALTON HAD BEEN sitting in a lawn chair next to his father for at least 30 minutes before an idea came to him like a bolt of lightning. He jumped to his feet and told his dad he would be back in a minute. He headed in the direction of the spot where he had met George Flynn and his family. He hadn't gone far before he saw them sitting at a picnic table. He walked over to them. George started to stand up.

Dalton told him, "Just keep your seat, George. I want to run something by you."

He sat down beside George on the bench. "Have you mentioned to any of the other employees that you met me?"

"No, actually I didn't want anyone to think I was —"

Dalton stopped him in mid-sentence. "That is great! Because I have a plan, and I need your help to pull it off."

Becky then intervened, "Do you want the kids and

me to go somewhere else while you talk?"

Dalton said, "No, I think you should be in on it, and the kids are too young to understand this move."

He told George and Becky that he was going to propose to his dad that he be put on the payroll as a beginning worker, assigned to George as his foreman.

"I want to be employed under a false name, and I do not want anyone, other than you and Becky, to know who I am. The fact of the matter is, I have been nothing but a big spoiled playboy, who has been accepting regular pay for doing almost nothing. And I want to learn, from the bottom up, about the company I will eventually take over. Dad says you are one of the best foremen we have, so I would like to learn from you. What do you say?"

George kind of blinked for a moment before he answered, "Give me a week or so to digest this idea. And I would like to discuss it with your dad."

"Fine, I probably need a week to get adjusted to the idea anyway."

When he left the park bench where George and he were talking, Dalton decided to take a stroll around and mingle. Nearly all of the workers in his age category had wives and children running around. There were couples in other age groups; some of the men looked as old as his dad. There were men and women who looked to be in their 40s and 50s, most of whom had older kids with them. In a couple of instances, older couples had young children, whom Dalton figured must have been grandchildren.

As he witnessed all the activity in the park, he thought to himself, *"I remember when I used to take part in these games."*

Most likely there are young men and women there today with whom he had played these games 20 years ago. He did not recognize a single face, and it was painfully obvious, none of them recognized his. As he continued his stroll around, he made a solemn promise to himself that he was going to change.

"I am going to give up my daily trip to the country club. Instead of golf and tennis to keep my body fit, I am going to start working for a change."

As he approached the shelter house where his dad was spending his time, he noticed his dad was talking with George. He walked up and joined the conversation. George had told the elder Heinkle about his son's plan, and Mr. Heinkle was thrilled about it.

Dalton said, "Well, Dad and George, I am going to leave right now, because I want to keep my identity undetected, if possible. I assume you and Dad will work out the details."

He left the scene. "I will see you in the morning, Dad."

The next morning Dalton was up and had eaten his breakfast before his dad came downstairs. His father came over to the kitchen table, seated himself and told the cook what he wanted for breakfast.

"Okay, Son, you have my full attention. You have come up with a noble idea, but do you actually think you are up to this?"

"Dad, I think I did more growing up yesterday than I have in the last 15 years. I saw so many happy families at that picnic. And I realize I have nothing but wealth."

"There's nothing wrong with wealth, Son."

"Yes, there is, Dad. I'll bet there is not enough money in all our holdings to buy George's wife. Or to purchase a couple of nice kids like he and Becky have."

His dad looked quizzically at him for a moment before he said, "I think you really have had a change of heart. You are serious about this plan, aren't you?"

Dalton answered, "You bet I am."

"George and I had quite a talk after you left yesterday."

"I figured you did. Is he willing to take me on as student?"

"Yes, he is. But he told me he would not do it for what he is presently making."

"How much does he make?"

His dad mentioned an hourly figure and an estimated annual salary, but with that statement, Dalton discovered another glaring flaw in his upbringing; he had no idea if George's salary was good, bad, average, poor or what. The only measuring stick he had to go on was his own unlimited cash allowance and his free use of a family credit card. He had no idea how much he would spend in a year's time.

Dalton said, "I want to start working at the same rate of pay any beginning worker in the plant makes. And I am giving my credit card back to you. I want to earn my keep for once in my lifetime."

"Whoa back, Son. Let's not get carried away. Do you realize you spend more money in a month than a beginning employee makes in a year? I don't think you can handle such a drastic change in your lifestyle."

Dalton thought for a moment before he answered, "Okay, Dad, I'll keep the credit card, but I am only going to use it in emergencies."

He then asked, "How much increase in salary is George asking?"

"He wants 10 percent increase."

"How much would that be?"

"About $5,000."

"Only $5,000? I think he should get $15,000."

"No, we can't do that. We do have other foremen, you know. George said he is willing to do it for 10 percent increase, so that is what we will give him."

"Okay, Dad, you're the boss."

A Different Look at Millie

IT IS A good thing they decided to wait a week before Dalton started to work for George. He discovered his wardrobe did not contain work clothes at all. He needed to go purchase some work clothes. He was discussing what he should buy with his dad when their cook interrupted.

"Excuse me, Mr. Heinkle, but I could not help but hear your plans, and about Dalton needing work clothes. Do you remember that my husband passed away a few years ago?"

Mr. Heinkle answered, "Yes."

She continued, "Well, Oscar was about the same size as Dalton, and I still have all his work clothes. I intended to give them to the Salvation Army, but if you think you could use them, you are welcome to them."

Dalton was confused by her offer. He hardly knew what to say; however, his dad broke the awkward pause.

"Millie, you are a lifesaver. It would be much better for Dalton to appear on this new job wearing older

13

clothing than in crisp new ones."

Millie then said, "Oh, there is something I forgot. Oscar's name is embroidered on all the shirts and jackets."

"That makes it even better. Dalton, you said you wanted to work under a false name; why not use Millie's husband's name."

Dalton turned to her and asked, "Would that be all right with you, Millie?"

She said, "Sure, it would; it would make me feel honored."

He told her, "I sure hope they fit me, because it would be an honor for me to wear them."

She suddenly pulled her apron up to her face and wiped a tear. Without even thinking, Dalton got to his feet and put both arms around her and held her tightly. As he stood there, holding Millie, he realized he had just done something he had never done in his life; he was hugging someone simply because he felt the person needed a hug. And it felt good.

Millie has been working for them for as long as he could remember. Mainly, she is the cook; however, since Dalton's mother passed away, Millie has been supervising the other two household employees. Besides Millie, they have a maid named Ruth and a groundskeeper named Salvador whom they call "Sal." Millie is about five or six years younger than Dalton's father; Sal is more nearly the same age as his father, which is 75. Ruth, the maid, could be anywhere from 30 to 50. Dalton rarely sees her. She more than likely avoids him; probably for good reason.

Millie said, "I will bring them over tomorrow."

"Why don't I take you to your home now? I can then find out whether they fit or not this morning."

She said that would be fine with her. So they went out to Dalton's car, where he opened the door for Millie.

As she stepped in, she said, "This is the first time I ever rode in such a fancy car."

He thought, *"Holy cats, here is another thing that emphasizes what a playboy I am; I have gotten so uppity that I feel it is commonplace to drive a Jaguar."*

Then the realization hit him, *"If I am going to do this metamorphosis, I will need to get a different vehicle to drive."*

He asked Millie, "What kind of vehicle did Oscar drive?"

She said, "He drove a pickup to work, but our family car was a Toyota Corolla."

"Do you still have those vehicles?"

She answered, "Well, I never did learn to drive to the extent I felt safe behind the wheel, so I gave the Toyota to our granddaughter, who is a senior in high school this year, but I still have that old pickup out in the garage."

Millie lived less than one-half mile from their estate in a housing development the company had established years ago. The houses were all designed about the same, and they were not very fancy, but they were well maintained. Mr. Heinkle had them built as rental properties for his employees; or the employee could also purchase the house. And there was a crew on the payroll responsible for keeping the houses in good repair. Dalton was aware of the houses, but he had never even driven through the development. He looked at the neat row of houses as they drove toward Millie's place.

He thought, *"These places might be similar in looks, but compared to the mansion in which I grew up, they have a glowing appeal."*

He stopped in front of the house Millie said was hers.

As she was getting out, she said, "I will be just a minute getting the clothes."

"Do you mind if I come in with you?"

She answered, "Certainly not."

All the Heinkle friends and relatives lived in huge houses. Even the so-called cabins on the lake were much bigger than any of these houses. Yet, when Dalton stepped into that house, he could see it was more than a house; it was a home. He looked around at the walls, and instead of expensive paintings with ornate frames, there were pictures of people. In the middle of one wall was a large picture of Millie and a man he assumed was Oscar. He stood looking at that picture. Millie entered the room with a box containing Oscar's work clothes.

When she saw him standing looking at the pictures, she said, "That was taken on our 40h anniversary."

Dalton asked if she minded showing him the rest of the house.

She answered, "Not at all."

Her house had the smell of cleanliness. It had one large living room/dining room combination, a moderate-sized kitchen with a utility room next to it. There was an arched doorway leading from the center of the living room into a hall and to the bathroom door. At either end of the hallway were doors leading into the two bedrooms.

Dalton thought, *"My gosh, two bedrooms and one bathroom, one living room and one kitchen. I think my wing of the upstairs in our house is bigger than this entire house."*

Then he asked, "Where is the garage?"

She led him to a hallway out of the kitchen. Off the hallway was a doorway leading to the utility room, which also contained a shower stall, a laundry sink and a commode.

As they went through the outer door, they stepped down three steps into a one-car garage that was attached to the house. And there, cleaned and waxed, was a bright red 1974 Ford 150 pickup. When she turned on the light, it looked like a new one. Dalton walked completely around it, as he slowly took a good look.

He asked, "Millie, would you sell it to me?"

She answered, "Well, I have been thinking about selling it. I could use the room out here. And I don't drive it, so it's not doing me any good."

"Great! I want it, and I will give you whatever you want for it."

She said, "I have no idea what it is worth."

Then he told her his dad would know. So they took the box of clothes and started back to Dalton's place.

On the way, he said, "As soon as we get there, I am going up to my suite and try on those clothes of Oscar's. I sure hope they fit."

She answered, "I will bet they are a perfect fit; unless the waist needs taking in a bit. And if that is the case, I will alter them for you."

When they walked into the house, his dad asked, "What took you two so long?"

Millie said, "Dalton, or I guess I should start saying Oscar, wanted a tour of my house. And it took a little longer than we thought."

"Yes, and Dad, she has Oscar's old pickup, and she said she would sell it to me."

"Great! Now that you have adopted Oscar's name

and will be driving his old pickup, what will your last name be during this training period."

Dalton said, "The old pickup is a Ford; I will be Oscar Ford. That will be easy to remember."

"What model is that pickup?"

Millie answered, "It is a 1974."

Dad said, "That makes it an antique. It should be worth about $5,000. Does that sound okay to you, Millie?"

Millie gasped, "Oh, Mr. Heinkle, that old truck isn't worth that much."

Dad said, "Yes, it is, and that's what you are getting for it. That is settled." He called the business office and ordered a check for $5,000 made out and sent to Millie, and told them to handle the transfer.

Dalton went to his quarters and began trying on Oscar's work clothes. All of them were washed, starched, pressed and neatly folded. While they were obviously not new, they were in very good condition. The shirts, caps and jackets were a perfect fit; however, the trousers were about two inches too large around the waist. He took the four pairs of trousers downstairs and told Millie she was right. The pants were two inches too big around the middle.

"It will be no problem to take these in two inches. I'll do it tonight."

Dalton turned to his dad and said, "You know something, Dad, I am really getting excited about this move. For the first time in my life, I feel like I am about to do something really worthwhile."

His father just stood silently for a long moment before he spoke. Then he said, "I wish your mother could be here today."

Dalton added, "So do I, Dad, so do I."

After a long pause, a voice came from the kitchen, saying, "She is, and so is Oscar."

The Transition

IT IS WELL that they decided to take a week to put the plan into motion, because they found there were a lot of details in changing ones identity and life style; even if the change is only on the surface for a temporary time. The first thing they decided; Dalton should not be living at home during this transition period. If he is going to be Oscar Ford, a beginning untrained employee, he certainly should not live in a mansion. Dalton asked if any of the houses in the development were empty.

His dad replied," I will check with my maintenance crew, but I believe the last time we talked, they reported having two houses empty."

It was not long before they were making plans to furnish one of the houses as Dalton's residence. They soon realized one week was not enough time to get the plan in gear. They calculated it was going to take at least two weeks. Dalton decided to grow a beard; he would have enough time; and a beard would help, in case there were employees who might recognize him. He surely would not be recognized by anyone while wearing Oscar's clothing and sporting a beard.

On the third day, his dad suggested, "Son, I think it would be an excellent idea if you were to take a vacation for the next 10 days while I get things set up."

"But, Dad, how would that help?"

He went on to tell Dalton about a company, owned by one of his friends, that was in a business very similar to theirs. He figured it would be very beneficial for Dalton to visit that company so he would not be stepping into this situation totally ignorant.

"Well, Dad, I am not totally ignorant about our company."

He answered, "Oh, yeah, what do we make? Do we have a foreign market? Are most of our products plastic or metal? How many employees do we have? Do we have a retirement plan for the workers?"

Dalton stopped him saying, "I get your point."

He did not realize the extent of his ignorance about the family business.

He shook his head as he muttered, "And I have a college degree in Business Administration. Boy, what a waste!"

The next morning Dalton was flying the company plane, headed nearly a thousand miles away. He had a briefcase containing a number of brochures about their company, and he had reservations in a hotel, along with instructions as to where he was headed and with whom he was meeting. He really did not want to take this trip, but he had accepted the idea that "Father knows best."

As soon as he was in the air and on automatic pilot, he opened the briefcase and began looking at the brochures. He looked at the first one on which he saw a picture of a riding lawnmower. The inside of the folder contained pictures of several different sizes and models; none of which were painted with any color; all they had on their surface was gray primer paint. Further digging into the briefcase revealed that the company made lawnmowers, chain saws, snow blowers and garden tillers.

It seemed the company was a contractor for several popular chain stores. The company name appeared only on a small aluminum identification tag riveted to the frame of each implement. The colors they were painted and the names appearing in the machines depended on the company for which they were being built.

Dalton thought, *"Hell, I'm surprised I even recognized any of these pictures of pieces of equipment; I have never used any of them in my entire life."*

His dad had arranged for him to have a complete guided one-man tour of an industrial lawnmower factory in Kansas. The mowers they made were larger and much sturdier than the Heinkle model, but the processes they used in the manufacturing of them were very similar. Dalton was very impressed, as well as being enlightened. He was there five days before heading home. His knowledge of plant operation was by no means complete; however, he was ready to start to work as a laborer.

When he arrived home, Millie was in the taxi that met him at the airport.

"Welcome home, Oscar. I am happy to know my nephew has arrived and will be living with me for awhile."

Dalton was a bit confused by this turn of events.

He asked her, "What do you mean, your nephew?"

She told him that she and his dad had come up with a plan that would put the final touch on the little deception.

Millie continued, "We felt if you were my nephew, it would be very believable that you would be coming to my place for a visit. And since you happened to be between jobs; and since the Heinkle Manufacturing Company had an ad in the paper indicating they were hiring people, everything would look legitimate."

She went on to say, "And I have a spare room for you. And that old Ford pickup your father bought from me is still parked in my garage."

Dalton was overwhelmed, but he liked the idea.

He said. "Sounds great to me, Aunt Millie. I am ready to move into that room whenever you are ready. Tomorrow I will go apply for a job with Heinkle Mfg. Co. I hear they make lawnmowers."

They took the taxi to Millie's place, where he would be living. When Dalton entered that little house and went to the small bedroom Millie had prepared for him, he was suddenly overcome with a flood of emotions he had never experienced. His chest seemed to tighten up; his throat and jaw tightened; his vision began to cloud up and he couldn't talk. After he had stood motionless for a moment, Millie came to him and placed her hand on his shoulder.

With a very concerned tone to her voice, she said, "Dalton, are you all right?"

He could not answer her.

She then came around directly in front of him and looked up into his eyes,

She said, "Dalton, it's all right. Contrary to what you macho men seem to think, it is okay for a man to show his emotions."

Dalton didn't know why, but he found himself actually crying. Oh, he didn't just break down and open the floodgates, but he had tears of joy streaming down his face. He reached his arms out toward Millie, and she put her arms around his waist. He pulled her close and hugged her as he buried his face into her snowy white hair. He could not understand this change with which he was overcome. He could not say a word for at least two minutes. As he stood there hugging that sweet old lady, he began to think he had actually grown up, even if he was a little late in doing so. Finally he regained his composure and broke the silence.

"Millie, it has taken me 32 years to grow up."

Millie then informed him, "I have taken the liberty, with your Dad's permission, to go into your quarters at your home and bring some of your clothes over here. They are in the closet."

He went to the closet where he found all four matching pairs of shirt and trousers Millie had given him. There was a pair of sneakers, a pair of sandals, three dress shirts and a couple of ties, along with a trench coat, a jacket and a few caps. She then informed him that his underwear, socks, hankies and sleeping wear were in the dresser drawers.

She added, "I figured with these things, added to the clothing you took along on your trip, you should have enough wearing apparel. And, by the way, I think you look distinguished in that beard."

Dalton looked at Millie for a full 10 seconds before he said, "Millie, or I guess I should learn to say Aunt Millie, I have never had anyone do so much for me in such a short time. I truly appreciate it. And by the way, if I were 30 years older, it might not be safe for you to have me living under the same roof with you; you do realize you are one classy-looking old gal, don't you?"

She actually blushed and said, "Oh, get out of here."

Then she quickly added, "Would you mind repeating that last statement?"

They both laughed. And he knew he was going to enjoy his time with Millie. He always did like and respect her, but this new situation placed her in a totally different light. Millie left the room, and he began unpacking his suitcase. When he had that task completed, he lay down on his back in the middle of the bed. The mattress was much softer than at home. It felt great. He looked around the room as he lay there.

He thought, *"This is real z … z … z … z."*

The Beginning of a New Life

SUDDENLY, DALTON FELT someone shaking his foot. He opened his eyes to see Millie standing by the bed.

"Come on; get up; supper is ready."

He rubbed his eyes. "Holy cow, how long have I been sleeping?"

Millie said, "What difference does it make? Go wash your hands; supper is ready."

Dalton headed for the bathroom.

He was thinking, *"Supper. I guess for the first time in my life, I am going to eat supper."*

As that thought went through his head, he could hear his mother saying, *"Now, Dalton, remember, you have breakfast in the morning, lunch at noon and dinner in the evening. People of our stature do not have supper; we have dinner."*

He said aloud, "Well, Mother, it looks like I am going to have supper this evening."

He went to the kitchen where he could see Millie

had everything ready. There were two plates, two big glasses of iced tea and several steaming dishes of food on the table; it looked as nice as it smelled.

When they were both seated, Millie asked, "Do you mind if I ask a blessing?"

Dalton said, "Of course not."

She reached across and grasped his hand. She didn't bow her head; she turned her face upward and closed her eyes.

She said, "Lord, Dalton and I are embarking on a new venture. We will be seeing a lot of each other during this period. So, Lord, we ask that you help us make a complete success of what we are doing. And, Lord, I know that you know our venture involves elements of deceiving others; however, we trust that you understand there is no harm, only good, intended in our plan. Now, Lord, we ask that you bless this food I have prepared this evening. Thank you, Lord. Amen."

He repeated, "Amen."

And Millie added, "When there are two or three forks beside your plate, it is dinner; one fork, it's supper."

He picked up the one fork and had a good chuckle for an appetizer.

That evening, around 7:30, the telephone rang.

Millie answered with a pleasant, "Hello."

She followed with, "Yes, he is here. Would you like

to speak to him?"

She turned toward Dalton and said, "It is your father."

He took the receiver and said, "Hi, Dad, how are you doing?"

"I am fine. Millie and I are going to get along fabulously. We had a great supper this evening."

"Yes, Dad, I really feel I got a lot out of that tour. I'm a long way from being ready to take over the company, but at least I'm starting to learn something."

"That will be great. We probably should not meet for awhile, but we can sure talk on the phone."

They visited for at least half an hour, and as they were winding their conversation down, his dad said something he had never heard him say to anyone.

His dad said, "I love you, Son."

Dalton was almost stunned. But his words did sink in.

He answered, "I know you must, Dad, or you wouldn't have put up with me as long as you have."

Again he experienced the same feeling he had when he first entered his bedroom that afternoon; however, he was able to regain his composure quicker.

He said, "Dad, I am going to try to prove to you that I love you, too."

They ended the conversation, and Dalton hung the receiver back on the wall-mounted phone. He just stood for a moment staring at the phone.

After a long pause, he turned toward Millie and said, "You know something, Millie, I wish I could have realized what a big spoiled baby I have been long before now. I don't understand why Dad has put up with my playboy ways."

Millie motioned for him to come sit in a chair next to her.

She said, "Dalton, I hope you do not take this wrongly, but I feel it is something you really need to know."

He could see by the look on her face that she was dead serious concerning what she was about to say.

She continued, "Your mother was a fine lady. But she was conditioned from the time she was born to believe she and all her family were superior to most people. Your dad wanted to enforce some rules on you, but she would not have it. And on her deathbed, she made your father promise he would always allow you to do and have anything you wished. She was raised that way, so she knew nothing else."

Dalton sat for a long moment before he answered, "I really appreciate you telling me that. I know it is true. I remember overhearing arguments between Mother and Dad over me. When I was 13 years old and refused to attend the annual company picnic, they had a real hot one; she also refused to attend. As a matter of fact, I think she never attended any more company functions in which workers were involved."

Millie continued, "No, she didn't. She was always nice to me; however, I would not have continued working for her, had your father gone first."

Dalton asked, "Do you think she loved my dad?"

Unhesitatingly, Millie answered, "Oh, yes. She truly loved your father, and he loved her. For the most part, they had a good marriage. She really could not help the way she was raised — any more than you can help the way you were raised. It is just so invigorating to know that you have discovered there are ways that have rewards instead of trinkets."

Dalton sat there thinking for a while before he asked Millie, "Is my sister like Mom?"

Millie answered, "Your sister, bless her heart, is almost a clone of your mother. And her life will probably run pretty parallel to that of your mother. The only difference is, your brother-in-law is not anything like your father. He too was born into wealth, so he knows no other way. Your sister and Fredrick are a good match."

Dalton said, "Well, that explains why Dad said he did not want to turn the company over to him."

Millie added, "He couldn't have done it anyway. Your brother-in-law will be inheriting a different business. As a matter of fact, I think he already has."

Dalton looked at Millie for a moment before he

said, "Aunt Millie, you are one hell of a wise old gal. I am so glad I finally came to my senses, if for no other reason than I am getting to know you."

She answered, "I am happy, too, because I must admit there have been many times when I would have given ten dollars for every minute I could have paddled your ass."

Dalton about passed out laughing.

When he finally quit laughing, he said, "We have done enough talk about me and my family; what about your family? Did you and Oscar have kids?"

She answered, "We had three children. We had a pair of twin boys who were tragically killed in an automobile accident when they were 15."

"Oh, that is terrible, I am so sorry. Did you know what happened?"

"Oh, yes, they were killed by a drunk driver. It was broad daylight; the boys were going to a Saturday morning school function when the drunk driver sped through a stop sign and hit the car on the passenger side. Our two boys and one of their friends were all killed instantly. The man who hit them was a known drunk; he too was killed in the wreck."

"I think I remember when that happened."

She answered, "You probably do. You used to play with my boys at the annual picnic. They were very near your age."

"But I had to attend that private school, so I didn't get to know anyone my age very well."

She went on to say, "Oscar and I adopted a six-year-old boy, whose parents were killed in a boating accident, and raised him as if he were our own. It is his daughter who has the Toyota Corolla I told you about. I have a picture of him and his family, along with all my kids, in my bedroom."

Millie got up from her chair, went into her bedroom and returned with several pictures. She handed Dalton a picture of the twin boys. He recognized them immediately. He did remember playing with the twins. The next picture was of the adopted boy and his family.

She said, "John is now 35, Lorie is 33, Suzie is 17 and Emily is 13."

Then she handed him a picture of a young woman and said, "This is our daughter, Peggy; she is 31. She is a kindergarten teacher in a small town in Nebraska."

Dalton looked at Peggy, trying to remember if he had ever seen her, but her face was not familiar.

After a bit, he said, "She must favor her dad. I have been trying to see your face in her, but she doesn't seem to favor you."

Millie answered, "No, she is a daddy girl. She looks like his sister Brenda."

"And you say she teaches in a small town in Nebraska. Does she ever get home?"

"Oh, yes, she comes home several times each year, and when she is not teaching summer school or going to college, she spends her summers with me."

"Is she married?"

Millie paused for a moment before she answered.

"No, she is still single. I am afraid she is too dedicated to her profession. She tells me she has no time for men."

"Well, maybe the right man hasn't surfaced yet."

Millie added, "She is very independent; however, she is happy with her work, and that means a lot. This summer she is doing some individual teaching. Her school has several kids who are falling behind, and Peggy is helping them catch up"

Dalton thought, as he looked at the picture of Peggy, *"Now there is nice-looking young woman; she is no beauty queen, but she just has a pleasant, wholesome look."*

He didn't say anything to Millie, but he said to himself, *"I think I am going to look forward to meeting this young lady."*

Then he asked, "Have you told her about me being here with you for awhile?"

"I guess I hadn't even thought about telling her. This whole thing came up so quickly, but I will tell her the next time she calls."

"How often does she call?"

"Usually once a week, but sometimes it will be longer. I usually do not try to call her, because she is so wrapped up in her work it is hard to catch her at home."

It was getting late, so Millie told Dalton she was going to get ready for bed. It was 9:30 p.m. She got up from her chair and went into the bathroom. He remained sitting and thinking about going to the employment office at the Heinkle Co. in the morning.

Peggy Enters the Picture

WHILE DALTON WAS sitting alone in the living room, the telephone rang.

Millie called from the bathroom, saying, "Would you answer that, Dalton?"

He picked up the phone, saying, "Hello."

The pleasant female voice on the other end answered, "Oh, I'm sorry, I must have the wrong number."

He asked, "Are you Peggy?"

She answered, "Yes, and who are you? Is Mom okay? Why are you answering her phone?"

"Everything is all right. Your mom is in the bathroom right now."

Her voice became serious as she asked, "Why are you answering her phone while she is in the bathroom, and who are you?"

"I am Dalton Heinkle, Jr., and it is a long story why I am here, but I assure you, your mother could not be better."

As he was saying the last words, Millie appeared in her bathrobe. He handed her the phone

Millie said, "Hi, Honey, I was hoping you would call."

"No; nothing is wrong with me."

"Yes, I am still working for the Heinkles."

"Yes, he is the same Dalton who has always been a playboy."

"No, it was not his dad, it was Dalton, Jr."

"Now, just be still a moment and let me tell you what is going on."

Dalton went on into his bedroom and closed the door. He figured Millie would be more at ease explaining the situation with him not there. A good 15 minutes passed before Millie pecked on his door.

She said, "Peggy would like to talk to you."

Dalton went back in the living room and picked up the phone.

"Hello again."

"I am sorry if I seemed abrupt."

He answered, "Hey, think nothing about that. I'm sure it must have been a shock to you when I answered the phone."

She told him, "I'm sure you do not remember me, but I am the girl who slapped your face at a New Year's dance at Capetties, so I hope what Mom has been telling me about you being a changed person is true."

He thought, *"Wow! That was Peggy."*

"Peggy, I admit I have been a complete —"

She interrupted saying, "Asshole, that's what you were."

He went on, "But believe me, I have changed; that is all I am going to say about it. I don't expect you or anyone else who has known my past to believe it until I prove it. But I do remember when you slapped me; I was wrong; you were totally justified in whacking me with a ball bat."

She asked him to put her mom back on the phone. Dalton went back to his room, but he left the door open.

Millie and Peggy talked for another 10 minutes.

He heard Millie say, "That's great! I'll be looking forward to it."

As Millie hung up the phone, she turned toward Dalton and said, "Peggy is coming home for a visit."

"Is she coming soon? What will she do about those kids she is teaching this summer?"

Millie answered, "She has a very competent aide. She is going to take a week off. She figures if she leaves her place on Friday, she can arrive here sometime Sunday."

"You mean she intends to drive all the way."

Millie answered, "Yes, that's the way she gets around."

"Well, heck, why don't I ask Dad if we can go get

her with the company jet? She could just meet us at the nearest airport where it can land, and that way you would have a lot more time with her."

Millie's response was, "Now there you go, back to your rich boy ways. I thought you were giving all that up."

"Well, this is different. And besides, I need to get in some air time in order to keep my license current. With this trip, I can get my time in before I start this new job."

Millie asked, "How would she get back?"

"Either I could fly her back or we could get the company's pilot."

Millie said, "I'll have to sleep on that idea."

First Day as a Common Laborer

DALTON WAS UP early the next day. It was Monday, and he intended to be the first one in the company employment office. He wanted to slip away before Millie got up, but he didn't make it.

She came out of her room saying, "You know what, I am going to take you up on that idea about flying out there to get Peggy. I wouldn't do it, but I know about your ability to fly that plane. I have heard too many people say that is the one thing you can be trusted doing."

He told her, "I guess it is one of my passions; and yes ,I am good at it."

She said, "Fine. I will call her and see what she thinks. If she approves, we will meet her in Nebraska on Friday evening; and I am going along on the trip."

"Great! I'm happy you decided to go along. Now I am heading for that employment office."

He went out to the garage to get in that old Ford pickup.

He thought, *"Well, here I go, a competent jet airplane pilot, who is getting ready to drive his first pickup. I hope it has an automatic transmission."*

He opened the door, got in the truck, turned on the ignition, and it started right off. It did have an automatic, and surprisingly, it was very easy to drive. When he got it outside and was started down the road, he realized it really was in excellent condition. It was clean and the engine was quiet.

He thought, *"Dad wasn't too far off when he insisted on giving Millie $5,000 for this truck. It is worth that amount."*

Then another thought crossed his mind, *"Did he skin her on this deal? Is this truck worth more than 5K?"*

When he arrived at the employment office, he told the receptionist, "My name is Oscar Ford. I am answering the help wanted ad this company had in the paper."

The young lady said, "Oh, Mr. Ford. I have a package here for you. I was told you would be in this morning."

She handed the package to him, and he opened it. Inside he found all the fake identification papers he needed to carry on the little plan.

As he was finishing inspecting the papers, the girl

said, "Mr. Ford, the application you submitted earlier has already been approved. You won't need to fill out any further forms."

Going along with the set-up, he answered, "Oh, ah, ah, well, that was quicker than I expected."

She then handed him an envelope and told him to take it to George Flynn In building #7."

She said, "Mr. Flynn will be your immediate supervisor. He will explain your duties."

Dalton took the envelope, drove the pickup over to building #7, walked in and started back toward a fellow who looked like George.

As Dalton was headed that way, George looked up and said, "Are you Oscar Ford?"

Dalton answered that he was, and George continued, "I am George Flynn. You will be working with me."

He extended his hand, and as they shook hands, George said, in a bit lower tone, "So you decided to really go through with it?"

"George, I have never been more serious about anything in my entire life."

"Good. Then we can get started."

"Oh, yes, I do have one commitment I have to fulfill before I can devote full time to the job."

George kind of lifted an eyebrow and said, "Oh? Then you are not fully committed."

Dalton answered, "Yes, I am, but I do need to keep my pilot license current, so I need to make a flight on Friday afternoon. After that, I can work an eight-hour shift every day — including weekends, if you say so."

The next three days were the most grueling Dalton had ever experienced. He did every kind of dirty job there was available. Mostly he did clean-up work and pack-mule work, but every task he was assigned was one which had to be done by someone. He was a common laborer. Fortunately, he was in good physical shape, so the endurance part of the job was not a problem; however, his hands were not callused and tough, so they were sore by the end of the second day. He found that those soft cotton brown gloves, the cheapest glove you could buy, afforded the best protection for his tender hands.

He asked Millie if she knew a remedy for sore hands.

She said, "Time and warm salt water."

By Thursday morning, his hands were so sore he could hardly make a fist. But George came to his rescue.

He said, "Today I am going to take you around to all the various machines in this division and let you watch the operators as they do their jobs."

Dalton thought about kissing him, but he didn't think it would look too great to the other workers.

Thursday evening he told Millie to be ready to leave for the airport by 1:30 p.m. on Friday. He would get off work at noon, hustle home and clean up, and they could be on our way. Millie had called Peggy, telling her about the transportation arrangement. Peggy taught in a town near Norfolk, so she said she could be at the Norfolk airport by 4. Everything was set.

Dalton had told Millie she did not need to take a thing with her, other than perhaps a sandwich or two and some soda or bottled water. Millie was really excited about the trip. In the first place, she was eager to see her daughter, but she had never flown in a small passenger jet and she was looking forward to it. She told Dalton his dad said he wished he could also make the trip.

Everything was progressing like clockwork. George let Dalton leave the plant early, so he had time to go file a flight plan before he went home to clean up. Millie was waiting when he arrived.

She said, "I went ahead and packed a picnic lunch for all three of us, so we could munch on the trip back. Is that okay?"

He said, "That is a great idea."

She also had a thermos of cocoa and one of coffee. Dalton hurried to change. Millie's excitement was beginning to spill over on him. He couldn't wait to get started. The sky was blue with not a cloud in sight, the wind was calm; it was a perfect day to fly.

Dalton grabbed the picnic basket Millie had prepared, and as he picked it up he got another reminder of how sore his hands were.

He said, "Aunt Millie, this feels like you have packed a week's supply of food."

She laughed and said, "Well, maybe I did put in a little extra."

They jumped in the old Ford pickup and headed for the airport.

Millie asked, "How do you like this old truck?"

"Oh, I love it. Oscar sure kept it maintained well, didn't he?"

She said, "He did all the maintenance work on it himself. He was a good mechanic."

Dalton answered, "I wish I could have know him."

Millie Flies the Jet

WHEN THEY ARRIVED at the airport, Dalton drove directly to the company hangar, activated the remote door opener, and the door rolled up exposing the company jet. It was one of the older models and one of the smaller ones, but it served the company's needs quite well. One of the airport attendants came over and helped pull the plane from the hangar. They loaded their stuff in the plane, and Dalton helped Millie in. He seated her in the co-pilot's seat, instructed her about the headset and helped her get it adjusted. Then he fired up the engines.

Millie asked, "Do I have to wear this ear phone thing all the way?"

He told her, "Remove it for a moment."

She started to remove it, but the shrill whistle of the engine answered her question.

She put it back on and said, "I see what you mean."

Dalton taxied to the end of the runway and waited for the control tower to clear him for take-off. They lifted off the Atlanta runway at 1:25 p.m. He could see Millie's fingers turn white as she gripped the armrest when he nosed that jet up in the air and pulled the throttle back. She never said a word until they had reached their assigned altitude and leveled off.

Then she said, "WOW!! This thing really sets you back in the seat."

Dalton asked her if she had ever flown before.

She answered, "Only a few times. Once in a small plane and twice on big airliners, but none of them were like this."

Then she asked, "Does this thing have a bathroom?"

He said, "Yes, it is pretty small, but it is right behind that door in the back of the plane."

She then said, "I came awful close to asking you if you had a mop on board."

She cracked him up again.

After they had been in the air an hour or so, Dalton said, "Millie, would you like to fly this thing?"

She said, "Oh, heavens no, I couldn't do that. I'm not even very good at driving a car."

He answered, "Getting it in the air and then back on the ground takes training, skill and practice, but flying it after it is leveled off up here is easy. See how I have this control in my hands. Now if I push it gently forward, the nose goes down; if I pull back gently, the nose comes up. If I turn it, like this, the plane banks and turns. Now, put your hands on the control, and just hold it while I move it."

She reached out and grasped the control.

He made a few simple maneuvers as she held the control. Then he released the control and told her do make the same movements — ever so gently. She made those moves like she had done it all her life.

Dalton said, "Aunt Millie! You old rascal. You have been holding out on me. That was a fantastic job."

She giggled like a teenager.

He was thinking, *"My gosh, here I am, flying with an old lady I have known for years, but until recently had absolutely no feelings about her. Now, I am having the time of my life with her. My, what I have been missing all these years! What a sense of humor this old gal has! And if I am enjoying myself with her, how many others like her have I shut out of my life because of that blasted silver spoon in my mouth? All my life I have had the illusion that I was better because we were wealthy. And I have associated only with the so-called upper crust. Now I have met George and Millie, and I find it is I who has the shortcomings. I have just finished a week of working with my hands, doing common labor. My hands are sore, but my spirit is flying higher than it ever has."*

He made a smooth landing at the Norfolk airport,

and they taxied up to the terminal where they got out of the plane and went inside; it was 4:30 p.m. Millie called Peggy on the cell phone to see when she would be able to meet them. She answered on the first ring. She was already on her way to Norfolk and would be at the airport within 10 minutes. Millie was so excited she could not remain seated. Dalton had to admit her enthusiasm was catching; he was becoming more and more anxious to meet Peggy. Millie was looking out the window when a car pulled into the parking lot.

"There she is," Millie said.

She started for the door. Dalton stayed by the window and watched a nice-looking young woman, wearing a brown business suit, open the trunk of her car and remove a traveling bag. Millie was hurrying toward her. He watched as the two of them greeted one another with warm embraces and kisses.

He thought as he watched them together, *"Golly, Peggy is certainly a much taller woman than her mother."*

He also could not help but think that he could not remember when, or if, his mother ever hugged or kissed him.

They came walking toward the terminal. Dalton went to the door to wait for them. As they entered the door, Millie started to say something,

"Peggy, this is …" But Peggy cut her off in mid-sentence.

"Oh, yes, Mother, I know Dalton quite well. Even if he does have a beard now".

Dalton extended his hand and said, "Hi. Peggy, it's good to see you." He wanted to say more, but he decided perhaps he should not push things.

However, he was thinking, *"She looked really nice in her picture that Millie showed me, but WOW! In person, she looks terrific. She is not one of those bony sleek model types like I have always been chasing. This young woman is sturdily built, and even heavy, by modeling standards. She is nearly a head taller than her mother. She looks like she could hold her own in almost any situation. But there is something about her that is taking my breath away."*

He then said, "If we get going, we can be back in time to have dinner together. That is, If it's okay with you two."

Millie said, "We would love that, wouldn't we, Peggy?"

Peggy responded, "Whatever makes you happy, Mother."

So they hurried out to the plane, loaded Peggy's suitcase and carrying bag into the baggage compartment and climbed aboard.

Millie then told Peggy, "Why, this thing even has a

little bathroom back there." She pointed toward the door.

Peggy answered, "Yes, Mother. I think most planes of this size have them; however, it is nice to know."

Millie suggested Peggy should sit in the co-pilot's seat, but Peggy said she would rather not. So Millie took the front seat on one side of the aisle while Peggy sat in the one across the aisle. Dalton showed Peggy where her headset was and explained that they all had to wear them so they could visit while in flight. They buckled their seatbelts and were ready for take-off.

After they were airborne 40 minutes or so, Dalton decided it would be great fun to pull a trick on Peggy. Knowing she could not hear what he was saying if he switched her headset off, he said, "Millie, don't look at Peggy; just act like nothing is happening. I turned her headset off. I would like to pull a joke on her."

Millie then turned her head slightly; she could see Peggy had removed her headset and was pointing to it.

"What do you mean, pull a trick on her?"

He continued, "You remember how easy it was fly this plane, don't you?"

She answered, "Yes, why?"

"Pretty soon, when she replaces her headset, I am going to ask you to come to the co-pilot seat and fly the plane while I go to the bathroom."

Millie said, "Oh, I can't do that!"

"Yes, you can. I will set it on automatic pilot. All you have to do is reach up and hold the controls as if you were actually flying the plane."

Millie caught on right away and was ready for the little prank.

Dalton then acted like he noticed Peggy's headset was not on. He switched hers back on, and she replaced it.

He said, "I'm sorry, I guess I accidentally bumped the switch to your headset."

After she had it back on for a minute or two, he turned to Millie and said, "Millie, would you mind coming up here and flying this thing while I make a quick trip to the bathroom?"

Millie answered, "Sure, I would love to fly it."

He said, "Just hold her on this same course for a few minutes."

She began to unfasten her seatbelt and move forward. She seated herself, reached up and grasped the controls. Throughout all this moving, Peggy was sitting straight up with her eyes wide open and her mouth open. Then, as Dalton got out of his seat and headed for the rear of the plane, Peggy said, "Mother, you can't fly this plane!"

Millie answered, "Oh, Honey, there's nothing to it. I flew part of the way up here."

Peggy got a very serious look on her face for a

moment; then she said, "Okay, you two. I know what's going on here. You set it on automatic pilot."

Millie released the controls and held her hands high in the air. They all laughed, and Dalton sat back in his seat.

He said, "Seriously, Peggy. Your mom did fly part of the way here."

He turned to Millie and asked, "Do you want to fly it again?"

She answered, "Sure I do. Take it off automatic."

He took it off automatic as Millie held the controls.

"Now remember; slow and easy movements."

She said, "I remember." She made the plane nose down slightly, then back up to level. She made a left bank and put it into a right bank. She leveled the plane back straight again. She looked back at Peggy and said, "What do you think of that? Do you want to try it?"

Peggy's response was, "Heck, Mom, if you can do it, surely I can do it."

The two exchanged seats, and Dalton went over the same instructions he had given Millie.

He said, "Are you ready to try it?"

Peggy said she was ready. But, strange as it might seem, Peggy's sense of feel on the control was not as good as her mother's. He had to take the controls back several times before Peggy was able to do as well as her elderly mother.

One thing about flying in a jet, it doesn't take very long to travel a thousand miles. They were back in Atlanta before 7 p.m. And they were all hungry. Dalton tossed Peggy's traveling bag in the back of the pickup and got in.

As Peggy seated herself next to the door, she said, "This truck looks exactly like the one Dad used to drive."

Millie answered, "It is the one Dad used to drive. I finally decided to sell it. Dalton bought it."

Millie continued, "By the way, there is something else you need to remember. While you are home this time, you need to remember not to call him Dalton; call him Oscar."

Peggy answered, "I can't do that. I won't call you Oscar; I will use your kid nickname."

He thought, *"Oh, Lord, she remembers that damned nickname."*

Millie asked, "What was your nickname?"

And Peggy answered, "Money Britches."

None of them said a word for a long moment. Peggy started to speak.

Dalton said, "Well, Peggy, I guess if a kid ever earned a nickname like that, I was the one. I really was a smart-assed rich brat. And I can see now how all the kids near my age must have hated my 'money britches' guts."

She answered, "Well, perhaps we were jealous."

He added, "No, it wasn't that. It was me, plain old 'silver-spoon-in-the-mouth' me."

He continued, "But I guarantee one thing, if I ever have a family, I will see to it that my kids are not raised like I was."

Peggy mumbled, "That remains to be seen."

There was another long period of silence before Millie spoke up.

"I'm not really hungry. I would just as soon go on home, maybe have a bowl of cereal later."

Peggy added, "I'm with you, Mom. I'm not hungry either."

So they went directly to Millie's house where Dalton told the ladies he was going to go get a hamburger.

He said, "You two would probably like to have some mother-daughter time without me hanging around anyway."

Millie answered, "Yes, we definitely need some mother-daughter time."

He told them he would see them later, got back in the pickup and left.

As he drove away, he thought, *"I don't think Peggy thinks much of me. I can't blame her. Now what am I going to do? I guess I will just go to a movie."*

He drove into one of those movie places that has

about six or eight different movies playing at the same time. He bought a ticket, a big box of popcorn and a large soda and went to a back corner seat.

Love Starts To Bloom

IT WAS 11:30 before Dalton got back to Millie's place. The lights were out, so he entered the house through the utility room and started quietly to his room. Just as he was about to reach the bedroom door, a soft voice came from the living room.

"Dalton, could we talk for a while?"

He stopped in his tracks. "Is that you, Peggy?"

She answered, "Yes. Mom is asleep, but I could not sleep."

He said, "Peggy, I don't blame you for feeling the way you do, and if you want me out of here, I will quietly leave."

She stood and came over to him, saying, "No, no, it's not that. It is I who needs to apologize. I was rude and inconsiderate. I didn't even thank you for coming to get me in the company plane."

He started to say something, but she cut him off, saying, "No, it's true. And I am sorry."

They were standing in the dark; with only a night

light and the light from a street lamp illuminating the room.

Dalton said, "Peggy, have you been waiting up just to tell me these things?"

She answered, "Mom told me if I was ever that rude again, she was going to turn me over her knee and blister my ass, even if I was a grown woman."

They both laughed.

They then went out in the kitchen. She turned on the light on the range hood and asked if he would like a cup of coffee. He told her not to bother, but she said there were still a couple of cups left in the pot, and it was still fairly hot.

He said, "Sure, I would like that."

Dalton sat down in one of the kitchen chairs. Peggy poured two cups of coffee, brought them to the table and then placed a small bowl of homemade oatmeal cookies in front of him.

He said, "Oh, Peg, I am a sucker for your mom's oatmeal cookies."

She sat down in a chair across from him.

"Do you know what? My daddy always called me Peg; that is the first time I have heard it since he passed away."

Dalton replied, "Well, I have adopted his name, so I guess I will just adopt his pet name for you."

She smiled and said, "I would like that, Oscar."

They both heard a loud whisper from around the corner in the living room,

"Yes!"

Peggy called to her mother, "Mom, you old fart, you have been eavesdropping on us all the time; you never have been asleep."

Millie joined them at the table.

She said, "No, I have not been asleep. I have been worried that I might have been too harsh with you, Peggy."

Peggy interrupted her Mom saying, "A person is never too old to be chastised by their mother, especially when they have it coming."

Millie added, "But I was really happy to hear you two talking like friends instead of adversaries."

Dalton said, "Millie, since Peg is here for awhile, why don't you tell Dad you are going to take a few days off. He can eat at the country club; he goes there almost every day anyway. If he needs something fixed, Ruth can do it."

Millie answered, "I have already taken care of that. As a matter of fact, your dad suggested it when he heard Peggy was coming."

Dalton told them, "If you need transportation, you could use my Jaguar."

Then he said, "I would like to continue this conversation, but I have to go to work early in the morning, so I am going to bed."

They said good night, Dalton went to his room, and Millie and Peggy went to Millie's room.

Dalton set his alarm for 6 a.m., but it was the smell of the freshly brewed coffee that woke him up. Peggy was already up and was fixing breakfast for all of them. Dalton took a quick shower and dressed for work. He went to the kitchen. Millie was now up.

He said to Peg, "I see you are an early bird."

She answered, "I find I do my best lesson planning early in the morning, so I always get up early."

Millie added, "She has always been an early bird ever since she was a small child."

Dalton said, "I am afraid I have always been just the opposite; however, I am changing that pattern, too."

They had a nice visit as they ate breakfast, no world-shaking topics, just plain chit-chat.

Dalton thought, *"Oh, how great it is to sit down to a meal without talking high finance, latest styles, country club gossip or current world affairs."*

He excused himself, saying, "I have to go. George will fire me if I'm late."

Millie asked, "If Peggy and I are not here when you come home from work, you can you fix yourself something for supper?"

"No problem. You two just enjoy being together."

When he went out the door and Peggy and Millie

both bade him goodbye, he was thinking, *"Oh, how great it would be to have a wife like Peggy; she is so different than any woman I have ever known. In the first place, I have always gone for the "cupie-doll" types. I have dated tall women, but I have never dated a woman like Peggy. She is large woman; I figured her to be 5'9", and she probably weighs 160 pounds; she is solid. She is also intelligent, articulate and witty, and, she doesn't take any crap off anyone. One of these days, she will make someone a great wife and mother to his kids."*

Peggy stood by a front window and watched Dalton back that old pickup out of the garage and onto the street. She waved, and he waved back as he drove out of sight.

Peggy was thinking, *"I just can't believe how different Dalton has become. I used to have a crush on him. I always wished he were not such a spoiled brat. Now it looks like my wish might be coming true. If I am not careful, he is going to light that flame again."*

.

Observing George

DALTON ARRIVED ON the job 10 minutes before starting time; George was already there. As Dalton went about his assigned duties for the day, he could not help but notice how George would talk to the men and women who were in his division. He never raised his voice; he was a listener, too. On two different occasions, Dalton noticed him pull a worker aside and have a short private conversation with the worker. During break time, he asked him why he pulled those two workers aside.

George said, "I never chastise a worker in front of other workers; and I never take more than one minute to correct someone who needs counseling."

Later in the day, George was informed by one of the people in supply that the delivery truck did not bring several items that were on the purchase order.

In a very calm voice, he said to the supply worker, "Is this something I need to handle, or can you take care of it?"

The lady said, "I think I can handle it."

He told her, "Great! If you do have a problem, let me know."

Dalton began to observe very closely that George's method of running his department was not that of a problem solver; he was a situation handler. Any time a situation began to develop from which a problem could evolve, George was on it before it had a chance to become a problem. A picture was beginning to form in Dalton's mind that he did not need to know how to run the machines or be involved in every facet of this operation in order to be the president of the company. As president, he could delegate authority to people like George and that supply lady and probably a hundred other individuals. One person cannot know it all, no matter how hard they try or how much experience they have.

That evening when he arrived at Millie's, she and Peg were gone. The first thing he did was go to the phone, and call his dad. He told him about how he had observed George's methods of handling situations; that he had decided no company could operate without competent people in several key places; and that those people should be allowed to do their jobs without a lot of supervision.

His dad said, "Ah-ha, you are beginning to catch on. However, you will also find there are workers who will crawl off in corners to take a nap; who will steal from the company; who will fake working while doing absolutely nothing and who are just plain goof-offs.

Dalton answered, "Yes, but that is where guys like George come in."

"Right again, son."

"Oh, by the way, Dad, did you ever meet Millie's daughter, Peggy?"

He answered, "Yes, I have, she has been here several times with her mother, but I have not seen her since she graduated from college and started teaching."

Dalton added, "You ought to see her now; she is really a great person."

His father remarked, "Her only problem is she looks like her dad, and she is as big as a horse."

Dalton cut him off, "That's enough of that, Dad. Yes, she is not one of those tall, skinny models. She is a big woman, but she is as nice, or nicer, than any woman I have ever met."

His dad came back, "I shouldn't have said that. If she is half as nice as Millie, she is a fine young woman. I hope I get to see her before you take her back to Nebraska. But I also hope you are not getting ideas about her."

His answer to that was, "Hey, Dad, she sure as hell isn't a social climber. You can bet your bottom dollar she would not be interested in me, but quite frankly, I wish she were. And for that matter, you might see a different person in Millie if you would sit back and take a real good look."

There was a long pause on his dad's end of the line before he said, "Son, I have taken a good look at Millie. She is a fine person, and she has been as loyal to me as she was to your mother, and yes, she is a nice-looking old gal, too. I may be 75, but I am not dead, you know. Yes, the thought has crossed my mind; I am a widower and Millie is a widow; I have thought about making a pass at her."

Dalton interrupted with a sarcastic tone to his voice, "But what would the members of the Country Club think?"

"I think we better end this conversation before we say something we will regret."

"You're right, Dad. I was out of line; I'm sorry."

His dad added, "It's okay."

Before they ended the call, his father told him he was really proud of the way he had decided to make this big change in his life.

He also told Dalton, "With your change in attitude, I have decided to retire at the end of this year and turn the company over to you. Do you think you can handle it?"

Dalton answered, "If I can make George the general manager, I am certain I can do it."

"George would be a great choice. He knows the business better than anyone else. However, in order to move George to that position, you would have to by-pass at least two guys in the central office."

Dalton asked, "Well, if you think my choice of George is a good one, then I assume neither of the two you are thinking about could do as well as George in that position."

Dad answered, "They couldn't, even though they are both college graduates, and as far as I know, George has no college training. He would still be the better choice."

"Dad, how near retirement are those two you just mentioned?"

He said, "One of them should retire, and the other should be fired."

Dalton answered, "That ought to get me off to a good start."

"Don't worry, I will take care of the firing. The truth of the matter is, his wife and your mother were best of friends; that's the only reason he is on the payroll. I might even enjoy canning his pompous ass."

"Do we have any more people on the payroll whose positions could be eliminated?"

"Yes, the first one would be yours."

He then continued, "I would guess at least 25 percent of the executive office staff could be cut."

Dalton thought, *"Good Lord, our company is as bad as the government about corporate welfare."*

Dalton finished the conversation by saying, "Dad, I think I have seen enough of the plant. I want to go there in the morning to have a talk with George. Then I want to spend a few days as a headquarters custodian. Most of the staff members don't really know me, and the ones who do have not seen me since I grew this beard. They never look twice at a custodian anyway."

Millie and Peggy were coming in the front door as he finished talking with his dad.

The Shocker

HE SAID, "HI, kids, have you two had a good day?"

Peggy said, "You are right, Mother; he is a first-class BS'er."

Millie said, "Peggy! I never said that, and you know I didn't."

Peggy added, "And yes, we have had a great day. And thanks for calling us kids. How was your day?"

He said, "This might well be one of the most significant days of my life, because I am finally comfortable with the idea of taking over the company when Dad retires."

He continued, "Peg and Millie, I have a lot to tell you after supper. I want your opinions about some ideas I have."

He told them he took a chance on them being there around 6:30 and ordered several pints of assorted Chinese delights, and they should be delivered any minute.

Millie and Peg both said at once, "Great! I love Chinese food."

The delivery boy arrived within 15 minutes. They sat down around the kitchen table and enjoyed a good meal together. Dalton then proceeded to tell them all about his telephone conversation with his dad.

Peggy said, "Wait a minute. Are you telling us you are going to work tomorrow as a janitor?"

He answered, "No, not tomorrow — the day after tomorrow. Tomorrow I have to meet with George."

He continued, "I have another idea I want to put into practice. You see, we have a lot of female employees, and I am sure many of them are young mothers. Right now we do not have a day-care center here at the plant; I want to start one."

Peggy said, "Now that is a fantastic idea."

Then she continued, "But it should not be for the mothers only; it should also be available for fathers."

Dalton answered, "I never thought of that. Thanks for the input."

Peggy asked, "How do you propose to finance your day-care center?"

He replied, "We would have to charge a minimal fee, but most of the money for equipment and remodeling should come from reduction of staff."

Millie entered the conversation when he mentioned cutting staff.

She said, "You do realize most of these people who work for your father would be in serious trouble in no time if they lost their jobs."

Dalton answered, "Not the ones I am going to cut. I am starting at the top. Dad said he would guess we could eliminate 25 percent of the upper echelon, high-paying jobs; starting with mine."

Peggy leaned back in her chair and said, "Dalton, I am beginning to really like you."

Then he said something that even surprised himself.

He looked straight in Peggy's eyes and said, "Those are the best words I ever heard coming from you. You want to know why? Because I am serving you notice right here and now, with your Mom as a witness, that within a year from this date, you are going to be my wife."

She was stunned. She sat up straight, opened her mouth as if to say something, but nothing came out. She blinked a few times and cleared her throat. She pointed at Dalton and again started to speak without saying anything. She took a deep breath and exhaled.

"I need a drink of water."

She went to the refrigerator.

Through all this, Millie was also stunned. She just sat there, saying nothing.

When Peggy came back to them, she said, "Dalton, you do not kid around about something as serious as marriage, and you do not tell a woman you hardly know; who also hardly knows you, that you are going to marry her — just like that."

"I'm sorry, I guess I was thinking out loud. But, Peg, you are real! You are … are … are … you are real."

He was also lost for words.

She answered, "Yes, I am real. I am real big."

He stopped her right there, saying, "Now, Peg, don't undersell yourself. Yes, you are not one of those little cupie dolls; you are not one of those tall, skinny models. There are all sizes of people in this old world; somebody has to help make up the larger size group. You are not a small woman, hell, I think you are probably an inch taller than me;. You might even outweigh me, but I don't give a hoot. You are different, you are honest, you are sincere and you are a caring person, or you wouldn't be teaching kindergarten. And, damn it all, I like you."

Now Millie entered her opinion, "All right you two, enough of this. Let's look at the facts. Peggy, you are 31 years old, right? Dalton, you are 32 years old, right? Both of you are single and have never been married. Neither one of you is ever going to win a beauty contest. Yet, at the same time, you are both neat-looking people."

At this point, Peggy started to interject something, but Millie extended her hand up to Peggy.

She continued, "Now hear me out, Peggy. After I have had my say, you may talk."

Peggy leaned back in her chair and Millie went on. "Neither one of you is a virgin."

Peggy said, "Mother!"

Millie added, "Hey, kids, I didn't just fall off the turnip wagon."

She went on, "Until the last week or so, I wouldn't have given a plugged nickel for Dalton, but I think he has actually made a turnaround. Peggy, you have always been solid. Both of you are healthy. And I happen to know that neither of you is involved right now. And I don't know about you, Dalton, but Peggy has had a crush on you ever since you were teenagers."

Peggy raised up at that remark and said, "Now, Mother, that is just not — well, okay, it is true, but he wouldn't give me the time of day."

Dalton said, "But I sure will now. I am not that spoiled brat any more."

He continued, "I shouldn't have just blurted that out. I hope you will forgive me and forget it — for the time being. However, if you are still not involved the next time you come home, I would be honored if you would allow me a formal date."

Millie interjected, "What's wrong with having one while she is here this time?"

Peggy added, "I think it would be a good idea. I have a lot of things I would like to discuss with you, on a one-to-one basis."

Millie said, "Good, we will make it tomorrow night."

Peggy was shaking her head and saying, "I just can't believe all this is happening. Things like this simply do not happen."

Dalton turned to Millie, "Do you have any sleeping pills? I think I am going to need something tonight."

Millie added, "I think I have about half of a bottle. We can divide them up; there should be at least four each."

They all laughed. Dalton started for his room, but Millie stopped him.

"Hey, you, I want a hug."

He stopped and said, "I really need a hug."

Peg added, "Oh, what the hell, we'll make it a three-way."

So the three of them embraced and held each other tightly.

Dalton looked into Peggy's eyes and asked her, "Are you barefooted?"

She said, "Yes, why?"

"Because so am I. And I am just about an inch taller than you. How much do you weigh?"

She answered, "None of your damn business."

They all laughed and went to bed.

Dalton lay there for a good ten minutes before he head a voice call out from Millie's room.

"She weighs 160 pounds!"

Followed by, "Mom, you old fart, I could paddle you."

Dalton laughed until his sides hurt.

It must have been two o'clock before he finally went to sleep. His mind simply would not keep still.

He kept thinking, *"This girl is almost a total stranger to me, and I am a total stranger to her. Whether we will admit it or not, we are both lonely people. Neither of us has had a meaningful relationship. I haven't had one because I have been too wrapped up in myself and too accustomed to having anything I want to be capable of looking seriously at anybody. And I'm afraid Peggy has been selling herself too short. She thinks that because she happens to be a little taller and a little heavier than the so-called 'average' woman, she is undesirable. My, how wrong both of us have been. For the first time in my life, I am genuinely happy; and for the first time in my life, I feel like I am a part of a real family."*

New Company Manager

MILLIE AND PEGGY must have stayed awake late, too, because, when Dalton got up, they were still sleeping soundly. So he dressed and left. He stopped at a little café for breakfast and then went on out to the factory. He was there nearly 30 minutes before George arrived.

When George came in and saw Dalton, he said, "What the hell are you doing here so early?"

He told him, "Because I need to talk to you."

He said, "Shoot."

Dalton went on to tell him all about the conversation he had with his dad. He told George he wanted him to be the general manager of the company.

"Now wait a minute, Dalton, I know there are two guys in the central office who are in line for that job when your dad retires and you take over."

"We talked about that. One of them is retiring, and the other is getting fired."

He answered, "I'll bet I know which one is getting

fired. He should have had his ass fired years ago. I think your Mom was responsible for him being here."

"That's what Dad told me."

"Anyway, what do you think about being the general manager?"

George answered, "Well, I have enough confidence in my ability to think I can handle it."

"Dad said you were the best choice for the job when I told him I wanted you to take it."

He said, "You can't imagine how good that makes me feel. If your dad thinks that way, then you have your man. I'll do it."

"Great."

They shook hands on the deal. "By the way, George, just because I am cutting my learning time with you off early does not mean you will not continue to get that 10 percent increase we agreed upon."

Dalton continued, "Dad is retiring on the last day of December. The new changes will be put in motion by that time. However, we won't say anything about the changes until I have decided how I am going to reorganize the central office. In the meantime, I plan to work as a janitor in the central office while I figured out what 'fat' to trim.

George said, "You know what, Dalton? I don't think I have ever known anyone who has made a complete turnaround like you have. You are all right, man. I am looking forward to working for you."

There was no problem getting Dalton into the central office building as a janitor. His dad found one of the present janitors sleeping in a storeroom, and he fired him on the spot. He phoned Dalton not long after he got home and told him to report there in the morning.

He said, "I want you to report to Gabe Johnson. He is an old black man who has been working for the company for years; he is a good man. He will show you what to do."

As he hung up the phone, Millie said, "Supper is ready. Would you go outside and get Peggy? She is out front messing with a flower bed."

"I thought Peggy and I were going out this evening,"

Millie answered, "No, I am going out this evening. I am going to go play cards with three of my lady friends. You and Peggy can stay at home and talk; go get her."

"I'm on my way."

When he got outside, he could not find Peggy. He called for her as he walked around the house. Then he saw her; she was down the street a couple of houses, down on one knee, talking to a little boy. He started walking toward her, and as he did, he could see she was so engrossed in talking to that child, she had shut out everything but the child. Dalton walked silently toward her and the boy and watched.

He thought, *"I'll bet she is one hell of a good teacher."*

When he got closer, she looked up.

He said, "Supper is ready."

She said, "Okay."

She gave the little fellow a big hug.

Dalton remarked, "You really do love kids, don't you?"

"That's why I am a teacher."

On the way back to the house, Peg said, "I guess Mom decided we should stay home tonight; I think she is getting a little bossy."

"Oh, no, she's not bossy. I love your Mom. I think — no, I don't think, I know — she is the coolest old lady in this whole country. If she says we should stay home and talk, then that is what we should do."

Peg added, "She is indeed a cool old lady."

Supper was on the table when they walked into the house. As they seated themselves around the table, Millie said a short blessing.

"Now, I did the cooking; you two can do the dishes while I go play cards."

They enjoyed the meal while Dalton was telling them about George Flynn agreeing to be the general manager.

Peggy said, "I do not know George personally, but his wife, Becky, was a senior the year I was a freshman; she is really a nice person. She never looked down on the underclassmen."

Dalton added, "I only met her briefly, but I think she is still a nice person."

When Millie finished her meal, she got to her feet, saying, "Well, kids, I'm off to the card games. I hope those three old gals are ready for a good whoopin', 'cause I am ready to play cards 'til midnight."

Dalton asked, "Do you want me to take you?"

She answered, "Oh, no, I am going only a block and a half. I like to walk; however, I will have Myrtle drop me off here when we break up the party — at midnight, that is."

She put on a light sweater, grabbed her purse and went out the door, saying over her shoulder, "I'll see you — after midnight."

Peg looked at Dalton and said, "I think she was hinting that we would have the house all to ourselves until midnight. Did you catch that?"

He answered, "I kinda got the drift, too. It is now only 7:15 p.m. Do you think we will have enough time?"

Peg said, "That is only four hours and 45 minutes." They both started laughing.

Peg continued, "How long does it take — to wash a dinner service setting for three?"

Dalton was amused, as he was trying to interpret her sense of humor.

Peg continued, "I wonder if she could have been hinting at anything."

Dalton started chuckling. "Is there something else we should do — besides wash the dishes?"

Dalton began to get tickled. He just couldn't stop laughing. Every time he would get hold of himself, Peg would make another remark.

"Mom is so vague. I wish she would just come out and say what she means."

He broke out again. He was surprised to learn she had such a great sense of humor.

After about 10 minutes of these giggling fits, Peg said, "I think we better have sex before we wash the dishes."

He realized she was only kidding, but it made him laugh until he started coughing.

She added, "Of course, we could do it while we are doing the dishes."

He could scarcely get his breath

When they finally regained their composure, Peg said, "You do realize I was only kidding about the sex. I don't think we are quite ready for that kind of commitment. And besides, I would need to know a lot more about your background than I know at present."

He told her, "I understand. And, of course, you are right; however, I think we should pull a good one on your Mom when she arrives home — at midnight."

"What do you mean?"

"I mean we should turn out the lights about 11:45 and watch for your mom's friend to bring her home."

"And then what," Peg asked

"Then, fully clothed, we hurry into my room, climb in bed and pull the cover up to our chins."

Peg agreed, "Oh, that is a great idea. I can't wait to see her face. We can fake sleep."

So they did the dishes and had serious talk for the rest of the evening. They were very frank with each other, and they did not skirt any issue; they hit everything head-on. Dalton really valued her input, especially on the female issues and the day care center. It was 11:30 p.m. before they realized it.

Dalton said, "I think we better turn out the lights, except for a few night lights; 11:45 might slip past us."

So they turned off the main lights and sat talking in the darkened room until right up midnight. That is when a car pulled to a stop in front of the house. They hurried in to Dalton's room, closed the door, but left it slightly ajar; then jumped in bed and pulled the top cover up to their chins. Peg was lying in a position to see the door, and Dalton was facing her. They heard the front door open and close. Then it seemed forever before they heard another sound. Finally, Millie came to his room door and slowly pushed it open enough to peek in.

When she saw them lying in bed together, she said, very softly, "Well, I'll be damned. I never thought she would hop in bed with anybody on the first date." And she started toward her room.

Peg yelled, "Mom, it's a joke! It's a joke!"

Millie said, "You sure had me fooled."

They got up, and they all talked until 1:30 a.m.

The New Custodian

DALTON ARRIVED AT the central office building at 6:30 a.m. As he entered, he noticed a black man at the end of the hall.

He walked to him and asked, "Are you Mr. Johnson?"

He laughed and answered, "Oh, no, I ain't Mr. Johnson."

Dalton was a bit confused as he said, "I was told to report to a Gabe Johnson. You are not Mr. Johnson?"

He chuckled again, but this time he said, "I am Gabe, but I ain't no Mister."

Dalton liked him from the start. He told him, "My name is Oscar Ford."

He extended a big hand and said, "Nice to meet you, Oscar."

"It's nice to meet you, too, Gabe."

He explained, "I have been hired as a janitor's helper; you are supposed to be my supervisor."

He asked, "Who told you I was a supervisor?"

"Mr. Heinkle."

"Hmm, I guess if Mr. Heinkle says I'm a supervisor, then I must be a supervisor. Follow me, I show you your locker."

The first thing he had Dalton do was start polishing brass doorknobs and railings. He showed him the polish and the rags.

He said, "It gonna take you a few days; they is lots of railings and knobs in this building."

Then he looked Dalton over and said, "Do I know you, Son?"

"I don't know how you could. I just came here from Nebraska last week."

He added, "You sure look familiar for some reason. Guess you just remind me of somebody."

Dalton did feel strange coming to work as a janitor in the only building he ever spent any time in at all. Meeting Gabe also made him think again about what a complete jerk he had been.

He thought, *"I probably have walked past Gabe any number of times, as I passed in and out of this building, but old 'money britches' never even noticed him. I just had such a ground-in feeling of superiority that I didn't consider people like Gabe existed."*

He went about his chores that day, taking mental notes of a number of things. One of his first observations was the designated smoking room. He never smoked, so he never went there whenever he was in the building. He did frequent the break room, because there were vending machines in that room. The break room also contained a refrigerator and a microwave oven, with tables and chairs and other furniture.

He decided to go polish the doorknob in that break room. Before he reached the door, he could hear talking and laughing.

As Dalton got closer he heard someone say, "We better break it up and get back to our offices; the old man is pulling into his parking spot."

Then someone else added, "I wish that old bastard would keep a more precise schedule. We could spend a lot more time in here."

Then another voice added, "Hey, I heard he won't be here at all tomorrow. Maybe we can have a poker game without worrying."

A different voice added, "I sure hope he is gone tomorrow. I am beginning to make a little headway with Janice; maybe I can coax her into the supply room."

They were all laughing as they started leaving the break room.

Dalton thought, *"Well, fellows, maybe tomorrow I can make a few notes. I think I am already beginning to locate a part of that 25 percent Dad was talking about."*

As they filed out the door, he realized they were all strangers. Either he never noticed any of them when he was in the building, or they avoided him, because his dad was the boss."

He also thought, *"I was a part of this element of jerk-offs. As a matter of fact, I was probably at the top of the list. How in hell did Dad ever put up with me?"*

Then he remembered Millie telling him about the promise his dad made to his mother when she was dying. The thought also occurred to him that it was not going to be an easy chore to weed out the deadwood; however, he knew it had to be done if he was to do some of the things he has planned for the workers. He spent the rest of the day polishing brass and making mental notes. He decided to just keep what he learned to myself for a week or so. He would start carrying a pocket notebook, so he could have a record of names and incidents.

About halfway through the morning, Gabe came over to him.

He said, "How you doing, Oscar?"

He answered, "Well, what do you think? Is that railing polished good enough?"

"Looks fine, but I see you ain't wearing them rubber gloves. You better go get some; them chemicals in that polish is not too good on your hands."

He reached in his back pocket.

"Hold on. I have a pair, right here."

He handed Dalton a couple of green rubber gloves, saying, "These is the best kind. They are hospital gloves. But you go wash your hands before you puts them on."

"Thanks, Gabe. I think that polish was beginning to sting my hands."

As he headed for the restroom to wash his hands, he thought, *"I think Gabe is the first black person I have ever talked to, and I know he is the first I have ever touched. How could anybody look down their nose at that old man?"*

Millie had fixed a sack lunch for Dalton, so when Gabe said, "Hey, boy, go get your dinner bucket, an' let's go eat," he did not hesitate at that invitation. He retrieved his sack lunch from the little janitorial supply storeroom.

Gabe said, "Just follow me."

They went to the end of the hall and then down a flight of stairs into the furnace room. Dalton didn't even know the room was there. Another black man, about 35 years old, was sitting at a table, opening his lunch box.

Gabe said, "Henry, this is Oscar. He is ole snoozlehead's replacement."

Dalton shook hands with Henry, saying, "I'm pleased to meet you, Henry."

As Henry shook Dalton's hand, he said, "A little advice from a fellow custodial engineer: do not allow Mr. Heinkle to catch you 'snoozling,' as Gabe puts it, while on the job."

Gabe added, "Henry here is one of them college grad-u-ates. He got himself a d-gree in en-gine-ear-in."

Henry added, "Yes, I have a degree in mechanical engineering. However, I have not had a chance to use it so far."

The three of them sat down around the little table in the furnace room. While they were eating, Henry explained the heating and air conditioning system. He was talking beyond Dalton's knowledge, but it was easy to see that Henry knew what he was talking about, and that he had a passion for his expertise. They wanted to know where Dalton came from, what he had done before coming here. He was stumped as to what to say until an idea hit him.

He thought, *"I'll just tell them I am a washed-out golf pro."*

He said, "Well, fellows, I hate to tell you this, but I am a washed-out golf pro. For the past 10 years I have been kicking around the country, trying to make a living teaching golf swings to a bunch of rattle-brained snobs at country clubs. I have made a living, but I was not happy. I decided it was time for me to do a little manual labor for a change."

Gabe asked, "Did you ever play golf with Tiger Woods?"

"Oh, no, he is in the big time; I was in minor leagues. I never was good enough to make a tournament cut; I was just good enough to fool some rich people."

He told them about overhearing some guys in the break room earlier.

Gabe said, "It is a shame, the way some of them so-called executives takes advantage of Mr. Heinkle."

He went on to say, "The truth of the matter is, they secretaries does all the work. I knows they is some of them dudes what couldn't wipe they own bottom, if they didn't have them girls to show them how."

Then Henry added, "That's right Gabe, and the real sad part about it is, the secretaries don't get one third the pay their boss makes."

Gabe said, "Yeah, an' one of the worse is that boy of Mr. Heinkle's. Why, that boy don't spend two days a week here. Fact, I ain't seen him for two weeks, has you seen him, Henry?"

Henry answered, "No, as a matter of fact, I have not seen him; he's probably off on a cruise in the Bahamas."

Dalton thought, *"I really hate deceiving these guys, but I am sure they will understand, better than most, what I am doing."*

Dalton asked, "Other than his son, how many more are there here who are not earning their keep?"

Henry said, "I couldn't say exactly how many, but I do know for sure there are five men who are shirking their duties almost completely, and there are three others who are not too far behind."

Dalton questioned Henry further, "If you know those things to be true, why don't you tell the old man?"

He laughed and answered, "Oh, sure. I can see the old man taking the word of a black janitor over some of his executive staff."

"What if I told him? If you tell me their names, I will watch them. Then when I have evidence of their work habits, I will tell him. You don't need to be involved at all, other than as my informer."

Henry never answered; he just said, "Hummm." And continued munching on his sandwich for a long moment

He then replied, "There could be a list of names show up in your locker sometime. I have heard of things like that mysteriously happening."

Dalton thought, *"Wow! How lucky can a guy get? Just what I am looking for is about to fall in my lap."*

Dalton said, "If a list should 'mysteriously' show up, I probably never would find out where it came from, would I?"

Henry said, "It is practically impossible to run down a thing like that."

The List

THE NEXT MORNING when Dalton opened his locker, a blank envelope was attached to the inside of the door by a strip if duct tape. He opened it and found two full pages of typewritten information, both sides. The list contained names of nine individuals, listed in order of their transgressions; the number one name being the worst and the number nine being the one with the least important transgressions. Number eight was Dalton Heinkle, Jr.

The first paragraph indicated the information in the document had been compiled by a combined effort of 12 "loyal employees." The last sentence on the fourth page simply said, "Good luck."

That evening, as soon as he. arrived at Millie's, he phoned his dad.

"Dad, I have information in my hand right now that is going to save the company many thousands of dollars."

His father was silent for a few seconds before he

responded, "Are you serious? How did you come about that kind of information?"

"The how is not important. The fact that I have it is very important. We need to meet."

"I am going to the club tonight, but I will slip away and take a Taxi to Millie's house later. I will be there no later than nine o'clock."

Millie was listening to their conversation.

She came to Dalton and said, "Excuse me, Dalton, but why don't you go get your dad and bring him here right now? I have enough food prepared for four of us. We can have supper together."

"Dad, did you hear Millie in the background?"

He answered, "Yes, I heard her. Good idea. You come on over right now. I'll meet you in the back circle drive."

"I'll be there in 10 minutes."

Dalton went out, jumped in the pickup and headed for the mansion. His dad was waiting for him when he entered the circle drive.

As he got in the truck, he said, "Who gave you this information?"

Dalton answered, "It mysteriously appeared in an envelope in my locker this morning."

"What locker?"

"My locker in the janitor's room."

His dad grinned a sly grin and said, "Well, you don't

need to tell me, I know who gave it to you."

He added, "I can't wait to see it, and I hope it is accurate."

Millie greeted them at the door, saying, "Supper is on the table. You guys can talk business after we eat."

Mr. Heinkle greeted Millie with a pleasant, "Hello, Millie."

Then he just stopped in his tracks when he looked up and saw Peggy.

"Is that you, Peggy?"

She extended her hand and said, "Nice to see you again, Mr. Heinkle."

He turned to Dalton and said, "Son, you were not pulling my leg! This young woman is absolutely stunning."

Peggy looked toward Dalton with a sly grin on her face, and said, "I resemble that last remark."

Then she added, "Mr. Heinkle, you are an old flatterer."

Millie said, "Come on, everybody, the food is getting cold."

They all sat at the table with Millie at Dad's right hand and Peggy at Dalton's right hand.

Millie said, "Before we start, let's all join hands around the table,"

Dalton reached out and grasped Millie's hand on one side and Peggy's on the other; his dad did the same.

Millie turned her face up, closed her eyes, and after a pause of at least ten seconds, said, "Thank you, Lord. Amen."

Mr. Heinkle asked, "Is that it?"

Millie answered, "That's it."

Dalton's father added, "Millie, that was the shortest blessing I have ever heard."

She answered, "A blessing doesn't have to be long-winded to be sincere. That one was sincere. Let's eat."

Dalton was well aware his dad was very anxious to see that paper, but he didn't show it. They had a nice home-cooked meal, spiced with good old family chit-chat; they laughed; they told jokes and they kidded each other.

Dalton thought, *"It's great to see Dad in such a relaxed, happy setting."*

During the course of the meal, Mr. Heinkle asked Peggy when she was going back.

She answered, "I was hoping I could be back in Nebraska before Monday morning. I have an excellent aide, but I feel I would be neglecting the children if I stayed any longer."

Dalton thought, *"Oh, nuts, I have been so wrapped up in this investigation, I forgot about Peggy having to get back."*

It is amazing how quickly one can become attached to someone, especially to a person as nice as Peggy.

Dalton told her, "I hate to see you go back, but I understand. I won't be working Saturday and Sunday. I can fly you back Saturday."

She answered, "That would be fine."

She added, "I hate to leave, too, but surely we can get together again one of these days."

Dalton emphasized, "You can take that to the bank."

After supper, Mr. Heinkle and Dalton went to the living room, while Millie and Peg were cleaning up the kitchen. They seated themselves on the couch, and as they sat down, Dalton's dad leaned over to him.

"You really have a thing going for that girl, don't you?"

He looked him straight in the eye and answered, "Yes, Dad, I have. She — has — everything! I mean Peg is head and shoulders above any girl I have ever known, in every way."

He just tilted his head a bit and said, "Hmm — takes after her mother, doesn't she?"

Dalton was a bit surprised at his dad's reaction to the situation.

He said, "Dad, I have learned so much in the last two weeks. And one of the most important lessons has been that money does not make the person. However, money can sure as hell ruin a person. I was almost totally ruined before I came to my senses. Since then I have met some REAL people."

"You really have changed, and I must say, it has been for the better."

"My change has been because of the people I have met; however, I made the decision I had to try to be different the night you asked me to come to the annual picnic. You were so serious that a tear was in your eye; it got to me. Then I met George and his family; then the real Millie came into the picture. She is so nice to me; and then there was Gabe and Henry. Peggy is the icing on the cake. I know one thing for sure. I will never again be a spoiled rich brat.

"Good. Now let's take a look at that paper you have."

Dalton handed it to him, and he began to read. As he read rapidly, he mumbled fast words. Then he would stop.

"Well, I'll just be damned — Charles Brennan. I kind of suspected something, but I sure as hell didn't know that."

"Oh, yeah, I knew Fred Bingham was up to something. That SOB is slick."

"Oh, boy, this stuff is great!"

"And here is Lori Johansen; I'll be damned. I wondered why she has been so cooperative lately."

Then he lowered the paper and said, "The best thing about this document is, I know this stuff is all right on the beam. There are a few surprises here, but there are so many that line up exactly with what I already know, the rest have to be true."

He mumbled a few more words and then said, as he chuckled, "I had a feeling that Henry was a sly one, but he is a lot better than I thought he was."

Dalton quickly added, "Now, Dad, I never mentioned anything about Henry."

"Don't worry, it is just between you and me. But this is a Henry exposé."

Dalton asked, "What do you think about making Henry our chief engineer?"

His dad answered, "Oh, I don't know, son. I know he has a great resumé. He probably is your man. I will have to admit, I should have put him in a much better position, but I was still too damned hung up with 'old school' ways."

He added, "This change in you is beginning to spill over on me."

Now it was time for Dalton to have a tear in his eye and a lump in his throat.

Millie and Peggy were finishing the clean-up in the kitchen.

Millie asked, "Do either of you guys want a cup of coffee? There is still some in the pot."

Mr. Heinkle said, "Yes, Millie, I would, if you don't mind."

Millie filled a cup and brought it to him, saying,

"Here you are, Mr. Heinkle."

As she started to go back to the kitchen, he reached out and took her by the hand.

"Millie, I know you have worked for my family for a long, long time, and I have always been Mr. to you, but I want that to stop, because I also consider you more like a family member. Would it make you uncomfortable to call me Dalton?"

She was a bit surprised, and she could not help but show it, but she was also a very sophisticated person.

She answered, "Why don't I call you what your father called you?"

Dad said, "That would be even better."

"What did Grandpa call you?"

Millie said, "D.J. And, it might take a little getting used to, but it won't make me uncomfortable. And, you may keep right on calling me Millie."

They all laughed at that.

Millie and Peggy joined them in the living room. Dalton watched and listened to his dad and Millie. It was so obvious that they had grown to be very comfortable with one another. Dalton was suddenly almost overcome with a feeling of euphoria. He was experiencing a family situation like he had never known. He was speechless.

Pretty soon, Peggy asked, "Dalton, are you all right?"

She rose from her chair and came to where he was sitting. She sat down on the arm of the chair and placed her arm on his shoulders.

Again, she asked, "Are you all right?"

He was choking back the lump in his throat.

He managed to choke out, "Peg, I have never been more 'all right' in my lifetime. I am sitting in the living room of a beautiful little home with my dad and two of the greatest ladies I have ever had the pleasure to know. Life does not get any better than this."

Peg put both arms around him and said, "You old softie, you're going to make me cry."

Mr. Heinkle watched Peg and Dalton for a moment before he changed the mood of situation with an announcement.

He said, "I have an idea. Tomorrow is Friday. You will be taking Peggy back to Nebraska on Saturday, Right? I would like the four of us to spend the day together. Does it appeal to you three that we all put on a pair of jeans or shorts and a T-shirt; get in my car, and just go for a ride in the country."

Millie and Peg both said they liked the idea.

Dalton added, "Yeah. Dad, that is a great idea. What time should we leave?"

Millie said, "Let's leave early. We can stop at some greasy spoon for breakfast; we can have hamburgers and French fries for lunch, and Lord only knows what we can do for dinner."

Dad responded, "Great! How does 7 a.m. sound?"

Millie added, "Six-thirty sounds better to me."

Dad said, "Six-thirty it is. I will be in front of this house at 6:30 a.m. tomorrow morning, hungry as a bear and frisky as baby kitten."

Then he said he had to go make a few telephone calls before he hit the sack.

A Short Excursion

THE SUN WAS just coming up when Mr. Heinkle pulled up in front of the house in his Mark IV Lincoln. He was early, so he came on in. Millie was at the door as he stepped up on the porch.

He said, "Well, Son, I have set the final trap."

"What do you mean?"

He told them, "As soon as I got home last evening, I placed a call to a friend of mine who is in the electronic spying business. I had him bring a crew to the office building late last night, after everyone was long gone, and they placed tiny cameras and recording devices everywhere; the break room in particular. His little cameras will send their signals to an unmarked truck in the parking lot, where videotapes will be recorded. I put a note on my office door indicating I would not be back until Monday."

Millie shook a finger and said, "You are one sly old fart — I mean fox — aren't you?"

As they started out the door, Millie told Dalton,

"Grab that picnic basket. I fixed a thermos of coffee and one of cocoa and four little bottles of water."

Dalton's father just shook his head, saying, "Women. They simply cannot go anywhere without supplies."

Millie answered, "That's okay, I'll bet you will be the first one to want something to drink."

Dalton thought, *"Oh, my, how great it would be if Dad and Millie would get together."*

"I left the keys in the ignition, Son; you drive."

So Peg and Dalton got in the front, and D.J. and Millie got in the back seat. They were off to the races. As they pulled away from the curb, Dalton had no idea what a great day he was in for, because he had no former experience to measure it against.

First of all, Millie directed him to a little restaurant at the edge of town.

She said, "This guy makes the best pancakes you ever tasted. And he will make them according to your taste."

D. J. said, "What do you mean by 'your taste'?"

She said, "I mean he will add peanut butter, blueberries, strawberries, mandarin orange; anything you want."

He said, "I think I will order a sauerkraut pancake."

They all laughed, but Millie said, "Don't order it if you don't want to eat it."

Dalton asked, "What do you order, Millie?"

She answered, "It is a surprise. Wait until we get inside."

Walking in the door, they were greeted by a big guy who was wearing a white apron and a white bandanna around his forehead.

He said, "Millie! My gosh, I haven't seen you in a coon's age. How are you?" Millie answered, "I couldn't be better, Pete. How are you and Margie?"

He answered, "Oh, I am fine, but she is as cantankerous as she ever was."

A voice from the kitchen yelled, "Let her be the judge about who is the cantankerous one."

She burst out of the kitchen and came to Millie. They hugged each other in a warm greeting.

"Who are these folks you have with you, Millie?"

Millie said, "Well, this is my daughter, Peggy."

Margie said, "Oh, my God! Peggy! It has been years since I saw you."

She embraced Peggy.

Millie introduced Dalton and his father, telling them, "Oscar and I used to play cards with Pete and Margie; they are old friends."

Margie escorted them to a corner table.

She said, as they seated themselves, "This one is on the house. Now, what would the rest of you like; I already know what Millie wants."

Peggy asked, "Oh, what does she want?"

"Two sweet corn pancakes."

Millie said, "I knew you would remember."

"Oh, yes, I remember. You are still the only person who has ever requested me to drain all the juice off a half-cup of whole kernel sweet-corn and mix the corn in the pancake batter."

They all laughed. Dad said, "Hey, I always did love sweet corn. Fix me whatever you fix for Millie."

Margie sat at the table and visited all the while they were eating.

Dalton thought, *"I never would have believed there was a restaurant with a friendly atmosphere like this one."*

It seemed Pete and Margie were good friends with every person who walked through the door. As they were leaving the restaurant, D.J. asked for the bill.

Margie told him, "Hey, when I say it is on the house — it is on the house. It was worth it just to see Millie and Peggy. And if you two are good enough for Millie to associate with, you have got to be good people. It's been a pleasure meeting you."

They got in the car and rolled away from the curb. They hadn't gone far before Dalton noticed a building with a sign on the front that read FLEA MARKET.

He said, "Look at that sign. I wonder if they sell fleas, remove fleas from animals or what."

Millie said, "You have never been in a flea market?"

"I never heard of a flea market."

His dad added, "I don't think I ever heard of one either."

"Well, pull over there. You are in for an experience you will never forget."

She was right. That flea market was more like a museum to Dalton, except that everything in it was for sale. D.J really enjoyed it because he saw things there he had not seen since he was a small boy. As a matter of fact, he purchased several items for his den.

From the flea market, they went to a Bison Ranch, where Dalton actually put his hands on the back of a live buffalo. The thing was so tame it would eat what the attendant called "range cubes" from Dalton's hand.

They went to a miniature golf course. They played four rounds. Dalton was amazed at how well Millie could putt. She won two of the four games; he won one and Peg won the other. Near the golf course, there was a go-cart track. They decided to rent four go-carts and have a race. Dalton had driven go-carts, and none of the others had, so he felt pretty confident he could win all the races. Wrong! Millie won them all. And at one time she told him she was a poor driver. But the rest of them all said she cheated. Her car didn't have nearly as much weight to move. Actually, she was considerably smaller than Peg, Dalton or his dad.

They went to a shopping mall, where Peg and Dalton got separated from Millie and his dad. They were about to go to the public address system for help before they accidentally found them; they were both wearing white ten-gallon Stetson cowboy hats, and they were not a bit worried about anything.

Peggy said, "Mom, we were getting worried about you two. We thought you might be concerned about us."

Mr. Heinkle answered, "Of course, we were not worried about you two. In fact, today is the first day I have had in years when I have completely turned off everything, except this day. I am enjoying myself more than I ever could imagine possible."

Dalton started chuckling.

"Go ahead and laugh. I don't give a damn. I have always secretly wanted a cowboy hat. I mentioned it to Millie when we passed a Western store. And you know what she said?"

She giggled as he told them, "I told him it sure is too bad he can't afford to buy one."

D.J. continued, "Then she said, 'Maybe if you go in and tell them how much you have always wanted one, they will give you one.' "

They ate lunch at one of those quick food places at the mall. They talked about going to a movie, but decided, since they couldn't talk to each other there, they would pass it up.

While sitting at the little table, eating lunch, they noticed an old fellow on the other side of the mall who was doing pastel chalk portraits of people while they posed for him. They decided to investigate. They walked closer, where they could see his drawings were quite good. They decided to have their portraits done. D.J. and Millie went first, while Peg and Dalton watched.

Dalton thought, as they posed for the picture, *"They look great together. And they look happy."*

While he was looking at them and thinking, Peg leaned close to his ear and said, "I think they look great, too."

That same feeling of euphoria swept over Dalton again, as he was thinking, *"I guess I am getting to be a softie."*

He got that lump in his throat and a tear formed in his eye.

The old fellow was a good artist. Dalton didn't know what his fee was for the two portraits, but he saw his dad hand the man a hundred-dollar bill. The old fellow looked surprised when his dad told him to keep the change. Their portraits were rolled up and inserted into a cardboard tube.

"I don't know about you kids, but I am ready to go to the car and just go for a drive in the country."

Millie agreed, "Me, too, my feet are getting sore. I need to sit down."

So they headed for an exit from the mall. There was a bench just outside the door.

Dalton suggested, "Why don't you old folks have a seat? We'll go get the car and drive by and pick you up.

"Great idea," they both said.

It was a fair walk to the car. On the way, Peg said, "Dalton, this has been a great day. I really miss my dad, and I know Mom will always miss him, but I am so happy she and your dad are having such a great time."

He took her by the hand and said, "I have never seen my dad this happy. I miss my mother, and I suppose Dad misses her, too, but honestly, the day we are having right now would have bored her to tears. She was truly a blue blood."

Dalton decided to drive off the main highway onto a blacktop county road. It was a winding, hilly road that led through the countryside, passing farmhouses and small villages.

Peg and Dalton were talking about the day-care center he was planning to start, when she reminded him, "You need to be very careful about whom you hire to run that school, and you need to —"

He cut her off, saying, "I already have the person in mind I want for that position."

She said, "You do?"

"I sure do. I want my wife to do it."

She answered, "You don't have a wife — remember."

"Yes, I know, but I have one picked out — remember."

Peggy said, "Now, Dalton, this day was supposed to be stress-free."

He said, "I know, I'm sorry. I can't help it if I am nuts about you, but I am. You take all the time you need to make up your mind,"

She interrupted him, saying, "I am pretty sure I am, as you put it, nuts about you, too, but I still need some time."

He never said any more. I just reached over and squeezed her hand.

All at once, they realized there was no talk coming from the back seat. Peg turned around and pointed to the rear view mirror. Dalton looked in the mirror where he saw his dad slumped toward the middle of the seat and Millie slumped over against him. They were both sound asleep. He began to slow the car down and look for a place to pull off the road. When he saw a big oak tree, he pulled off the road and under the tree.

He stopped, and said, "Peg, come over here to me; let's take a nap, too."

She scooted over to him; he put his arm around

her, and they kissed — for the first time.

She looked into his eyes and said, "Dalton, you really are a nice guy. It might be easy to learn to love you."

He just hugged her tightly. He looked at his watch. It was 1:45 p.m.

The Old Courthouse

SUDDENLY DALTON WAS awakened by the sound of a big truck, as it roared past their position. Peg also was aroused.

Dalton said, "My gosh, we did fall asleep."

At the same time, D.J. and Millie were sitting up straight.

"What the hell — did we fall asleep?"

"You and Millie were taking a nap, so I pulled off the road under this big oak tree. I guess Peg and I fell asleep, too."

Millie asked, "Where are we?"

"We are on a county road, and we have been napping for two hours."

Dalton looked at his watch; it read 3:45 p.m.

D.J. said, "I feel refreshed, but I need to find a bathroom."

"There is a town down the road a mile or so; I can see the grain silos."

So Dalton pulled back on the road and headed

toward the silos. When they reached the town, they pulled into a Casey's store. They all needed to make a pit stop and have something to drink. Dalton had never been in a Casey's or any other convenience store. He was amazed at the amount and the variety of stock on display.

Leaving the Casey store, they headed toward the town square. Situated in the center of the square was an old red brick building; Millie said it was the "courthouse." The building was three stories tall, and it had tall spires extending high in the air.

Dalton said, "I wonder if we would be allowed to go inside."

Millie answered, "Of course, you may; this belongs to the residents of the county. It is open to the public."

"Then I want to go inside and look around."

Peggy said she had never been in such a beautiful old building, so they all got out of the car and started walking up the sidewalk. The outside steps were made of stone, but each step was worn down from years of use. There was a plaque by the door, indicating the building was constructed in 1893.

Dalton said, "Holy cow! This building is over 100 years old."

Inside, they discovered the floors were wooden, and they creaked as they walked on them. While they were looking around the main lobby, a lady approached them.

"I'll bet you folks are just passing through. Would you like a guided tour of our courthouse?"

They said we would be delighted.

For the next 30 minutes, the lady guide took them from the basement where the old jail cells were still intact, but now used for storage, to the third floor where the county commissioners met twice each month and where the courtroom was located.

She showed them the county office rooms and introduced them to the elected official, when they were there. When the tour was nearly completed, D.J. started to tip the lady and asked if she was the official tour guide all the time.

She answered, "Oh, heavens no. I just happened to be here today filing a document, and I noticed you folks. I figured you were from out of town, so I thought I would be neighborly and show you around. And I wouldn't think of taking money from you for doing something I enjoy doing. We are all proud of our old courthouse."

Dalton thought, *"Is there no end to the depth of my ignorance? I never would have believed people like this lady existed."*

As they started to leave the old courthouse, Millie asked the nice lady, "Is there a good restaurant here in town you would recommend?"

The lady answered, "Oh, heavens yes, we have several excellent restaurants. As a matter of fact, if you will take a peek right over my left shoulder, you will be looking at one of our finest."

They all looked in the direction she indicated. They could see the neon sign of a restaurant on the corner, not 100 feet from where they had parked.

Millie said, "Thank you. And what is your name?"

The lady said, "Here, allow me to give you one of my business cards."

She handed Millie her card and left. Millie looked at the card and started chuckling.

"Listen to this: Judy R. Lindquist, Attorney — Lindquist, Barber and Thompson, All Lady Law Firm, The Best Legal Beavers in the County."

Dalton and his dad started laughing so hard his dad had to sit down on the steps.

Peggy asked, "What is so funny?"

Millie turned to her. "A beaver is a male slang term for (she whispered a word in Peggy's ear)."

Peggy, too, had to take a seat beside D.J.. They were still laughing when they entered the restaurant.

The restaurant was divided into two sections. The section nearest the door looked like an average eating establishment; however, the rear section looked like it was set up for a banquet; with white linen table covers, linen napkins, stemmed glasses, flowers and candles. A girl asked which section they preferred.

D.J. turned to the ladies. "You girls decide."

Peggy said, "The dining room."

They had an excellent meal, with excellent service.

When D.J. looked at the check, he said, "My country cub could not have served a better dinner, even at their best, and the check would have been at least three times this amount."

Dalton said, "I knew that, Dad. That's why, when you informed us this morning you were paying all the expenses, I didn't argue about it. I figured you could afford these rates."

D.J. threw his napkin across the table at Dalton.

It was dark by the time they left the restaurant.

"Give me the keys. I had a good nap, so I am refreshed and ready to drive home."

Dalton handed him the keys, Peg and Dalton got in the back seat, and Millie seated herself next to D.J.

"Does anybody know what direction I should go in order to get us home?"

Millie chided him. "You men! It's a good thing we women are around; you guys would get lost going to the corner for a quart of milk." .

"Now, that statement is true. I didn't even know we had a corner store."

On the way home, Peg and Dalton made the plans for her trip back to Nebraska. They decided there was no particular hurry. They really didn't need to leave before noon. Dalton would still have time to fly back home before it got too late.

With that settled, Peg asked him, "Have you ever known someone with AIDS?"

He thought for a moment before he answered. "No, I never have. I have discussed AIDS with many of my friends, but nobody in my little aristocratic circle seemed to really give a damn. Oh, we were aware of the dangers, and I, for one, always used protection."

Then he added, "However, I must admit, my main concern was, I didn't want to get some girl pregnant."

Peg told him she personally knew two girls who died of AIDS.

He said, "Were they close friends?"

She answered, "Yes. Both of them were college classmates. One of them got it from her husband, after five years of marriage."

"Oh, God, that is terrible."

She went on, "The other friend caught it during spring break in Florida; she didn't realize she had it for eight years."

They just sat and held hands for several miles.

Dalton broke the silence with, "Have you ever been tested?"

She said, "Yes, I had a fling with a guy a couple of years ago. After we broke up, I started worrying; so I got tested. I am clear."

"You know something, Peg? Most people assume that a rich guy, who drives a Jag and has everything he wants, is sleeping with a different girl every night. It's not true; at least, it's not true in my case."

She gave him a little shove and said, "Oh, get out of here."

He insisted, "No, I'm not kidding. Oh, I admit I have had 'flings,' as you put it. I went with one girl for more than a year, but I could count all my encounters on my fingers — not including my thumbs."

She thought for a moment, and then she said, "You have me beat by two."

Dalton really cracked up, and then so did she.

Millie raised her voice, as she said, "Okay, what's going on back there?"

Peg said, "We're having a contest, Mom."

Then Dalton really lost it.

Before long, they were in front of Millie's house.

Dalton turned to Peg. "I think I am going home with Dad tonight. I have some things I need to discuss with him."

She answered, "I think you should. I have some things I need to discuss with Mom, too."

He gave her a good night kiss, and she got out of the car. His dad was getting out of the car. He walked around to the other side, where he extended his elbow to Millie. She took his arm, and he walked her to the

125

door; Peggy had already gone in the house. Dalton watched the silhouette of his dad and Millie as they stood facing each other. He could not hear them. They stood face to face with one another for a moment, and then his dad reached his hands out and took Millie's hands in his. He leaned forward and kissed her. Again Dalton felt that flood of emotion surge through his body, as tears of happiness rolled down his cheeks.

He had moved to the driver's seat before his dad returned to the car. He entered the passenger side; Dalton started the car moving;

The elder Heinkle just sat there for several blocks before he said, "Son, those two women are two of the nicest individuals I have ever met. I can readily see why you love that Peggy. I have enjoyed this day more than I ever could have imagined possible."

"Me, too, Dad. Remember when I told you Peggy was real."

"Yes, I remember; you are definitely right; she is real."

He went on to say, "I have known for years that Millie is, 'real,' as you put it. I always liked and re-spected her, but I saw a different Millie today; I hesi-tate to say this to you, Son, but Millie made me feel more alive today than your mother ever made me feel."

"Dad, I loved Mom, but I knew the two of you were never really happy. She was more interested in high society than anything else."

"What would you think if I asked Millie to marry me?"

"The only thing that would give me a bigger thrill would be to hear Peg tell me she would marry me."

Dalton added, "You are 75 years old, Dad, and Millie must be at least 70."

Dad said, "She is 72."

"Well, then what the hell are you waiting for? Grab how ever many years of happiness you have left."

As soon as they got home, his dad went straight to the telephone and called Millie.

He said, "Peggy, I need to speak with your mother."

He waited until Millie came to the phone.

"Millie, I have something serious to talk to you about. In the first place, I know full well the difference between our bank accounts is considerable, and I realize you are probably more aware of that fact than I. However, I discovered today that financial holdings do not have a damn thing to do with happiness. Personal relationships are the seeds of happiness. I have also discovered today that you can be acquainted with a person for years and not really know them. Today I got to know you as a person."

He took a deep breath and continued, "Millie, I have never had a more enjoyable day in my entire life. I am 75 and you are 72. We don't have a hell of a lot of years left to be happy. I was wondering if you — you will? Hell, I haven't even asked you yet."

"Yes, I do realize you probably know me better than I know myself."

"Okay, we will work out the arrangements tomorrow. Good night, and sweet dreams. I know I am going to have some."

He turned to Dalton and said, "I'll just be damned. I thought that was going to be difficult."

And then he yelled, "Yeeee-haaaa" and gave Dalton the biggest bear hug he'd ever had.

Dalton thought, *"I hope Peg will be that easy to convince."*

They went to bed.

Peg's Proposal

DALTON WOKE UP to the sound of the telephone ringing.

"Hello. Hi, Peg … I will get Dad up … we can be there in 30 minutes."

Dalton went to wake his dad, but found him up and dressed.

He asked, "Who was that?"

"That was Peg. They want us to come over for breakfast."

He said, "Well, come on, slow poke, Get a move on. If you're not ready in 10 minutes, you're going to walk."

They were there in 15 minutes. Peggy met them at the door.

"Dalton, I want you to know, I am giving you fair notice, with your dad and my mom as witnesses, you are going to be my husband by this time next year."

Dalton grabbed her and held her so tight his arms started aching.

He said, "Peg, I guarantee you are not going to regret your decision. I knew I loved you from the minute I saw you."

This time it was his dad who was stunned. He still had a slack jaw when Dalton finished telling him that he had made that same speech to Peg earlier.

"It took her a little longer to answer than it did her mother."

Millie said, "Breakfast is ready."

They all sat down at the kitchen table.

This time Dalton said, "I want to give thanks."

He turned his face upward, the same as Millie did, and said, "Lord, this is the first time I have ever done this, but here goes. I don't know if you have had a hand in this last turn of events or not, but if you did, I want you to know how truly grateful I am. I am certain, in my own mind, that Dad and Millie are going to finish out their remaining years in true happiness; and I promise you that I am going to be a loving, devoted husband to Peg — that's all I have to say. Amen."

Then he said, "It just occurred to me that from now on, Millie, you are not 'Aunt Millie,' you are Mom. If that's all right with you."

Then Peg said, "May I call you Dad, Mr. Heinkle?" He never answered; he just reached over and hugged her and kissed her on the cheek.

Dalton took a drink of coffee to wash down the

lump in his throat.

He thought, *"Why couldn't this have happened much sooner?"*

The Wedding

THE NEXT MORNING when he came home from filing the Nebraska flight plan, his dad was dressed in a business suit and waiting.

He said, "Go get your suit on. We are picking Millie and Peggy up in 30 minutes."

"What's going on, Dad?"

He answered, "I have arranged for all of us to appear before Judge Hemmingway at 10:30 this morning. Tonight, the sun will set on Mr. and Mrs. Dalton J. Heinkle, Sr. Peggy and you will be best man and bridesmaid."

He asked, "But what about the marriage license? This is Saturday."

"You think I could not handle a minor detail like that?"

Then he added, "Millie and I are not going to experience another moment of loneliness."

They all entered Judge Hemmingway's chamber

promptly at 10:30 a.m. The ceremony was short and simple.

Millie had insisted, "At our ages, there is no need for new wedding rings; they are nothing but a symbol anyway."

She said, "We can keep on wearing the ones our fingers are accustomed to wearing. I am sure our deceased spouses will not object."

Dad agreed. He said, "The important thing is the commitment. I am retiring soon, and my new bride and I are going to take one day at a time; but we are doing it together."

As they were leaving the judge's chamber, Peg said to Dalton, "I am thrilled to death that our parents have found each other, and their wedding ceremony was nice; however, it will be our first. I would like a more formal wedding, if that is all right with you."

Dalton squeezed her arm to his side and said, "Peggy, I want you to have exactly the wedding you have in mind. All I know is that I will take you any way I can get you."

D.J. and Millie decided they had better things to do than take a plane ride to Nebraska and back. So Peg and Dalton took off at 1:30 p.m. She sat in the co-pilot's seat, and they talked into the little microphones and listened with their padded ear speakers. They laughed, they shed a few tears of happiness, and they planned their future together.

Dalton would soon be the president of Heinkle Manufacturing Inc., and she would soon be the director of our new children's services program. Mr. Heinkle decided to sell the Heinkle Mansion. D.J. and Millie would live in the house Millie had occupied, and Peg an Dalton would move into one of the vacant ones. Peg would fulfill her present obligation as a summer school teacher; however, she would resign from her regular teaching contract and make plans for an October wedding.

Dalton was not a singer by any stretch of the imagination, and there are very few songs of which he knew the words. However, not long after he met Peggy, he heard one that he liked so well, he learned the words.

He started singing, "I'm happy standing in these shoes; with you here in my life; the world is looking bright on this side of the moon."

Peggy said, "I love that song. Shall we have it sung at our wedding?"

Dalton answered, "Mention that to Dad; he might have Alabama there to sing it in person."

Dalton didn't want to leave Peg in Nebraska, but he knew she had a lot of things to wrap up before she could be with him permanently. And he, too, had some very serious decisions to make before his dad retired. He held her tightly and promised he would come to see her every chance he got.

She said, "I know, Dalton. This has been such a whirlwind week that my head is still spinning. I don't want you to leave either, but we both have things to do. So get the hell out of here before I decide to talk you into staying tonight."

He answered, "Oh, don't even mention it. I would be an easy mark."

They said goodbye and Dalton went back to his plane.

The Axe Falls

THE NEXT MORNING Dalton's father told him, "I have called a meeting today with all the individuals who are affected by our next move. I will start the meeting, and then I want you to appear in your janitor's work clothes, at which time we will drop the bomb.

Dalton said, "I can hardly wait."

His dad added, "I will have the others report at 8 p.m.; you appear at 8:15."

When Mr. Heinkle entered, the boardroom was buzzing with small talk as the "guests" were availing themselves of the customary coffee and donuts, while they milled around, visiting one another. No one suspected what was to come. Promptly at 8:15, Dalton walked into the room wearing Oscar's Dickie pants and shirt. The only difference in his appearance was that he had shaved off his beard in the janitor's room before he went to the meeting. At first, most of them just thought he was coming in to clean something or bring more goodies, but when he walked to the front of the room and stood by his dad, they began to realize who he was. You could hear a pin drop.

Dalton heard a voice in the back say, "My God, that janitor is his kid."

Mr. Heinkle did not need to ask for their attention; they were all smart enough to realize something serious was about to take place. He stood, in that deathly silence, for a full minute before he spoke.

"Gentlemen — and lady — I have good news — and I have bad news. The good news is, this company is making some positive changes; however, the bad news is — none of you will be around to notice them. You are all fired! You will receive two months' pay; however, I am giving you only 24 hours to remove all of your belongings from this building."

At this point, one of them said, "You can't do this! We will all sue you."

"Oh, yes, there is something else."

He turned on the VCR and directed their attention to the large screen in the back of the boardroom. He allowed the tape to run for about three minutes before he shut it off.

Everybody looked shocked and bewildered, as he said, "You see that stack of tapes on that table? You may each have a copy if you wish; the original is in safekeeping. After you view the tape, if you feel you have reason to contest your being fired, please inform us as to who will be representing you in court."

Then a voice from the back said, "What about your kid? Is he getting the axe, too?"

"No, he isn't getting the axe; he got it a month ago. Would any of you like to apply for a janitor's position? You may work with Gabe as your boss, just like he has been doing."

Mr. Heinkle's last words to that group were, "Many of you have worked for me for years. I assumed you were loyal, since all of our face-to-face encounters were pleasant. As I began to get older, I guess you assumed I would also get senile. Well, I didn't. I did get soft, and I trusted you. You took advantage of me, and it has hurt me to know you were not my friends. I have some advice for you — wherever you go from here, whatever you do, for whomever you work. Don't do it again to someone else. Good bye, and good luck."

He turned and left the room. As those 11 individuals filed silently out of the room, Dalton could not help but feel sorry for them.

He thought, *"What have I done? Do they really deserve this treatment? After all, I was number eight on the list. Did they do it because they knew I was getting away it? Looks like I have a wrestling match scheduled with my own conscience."*

That night he went to Millie's house, and to the

simple room he had grown to love. He called Peggy as he was fixing himself a cup of coffee.

He said, "Peg, I need your counseling. Dad fired 11 executives today, and as they left that room, with heads low, I wondered if I had done the right thing."

She answered, "Now, Dalton, do not get to thinking that way! You did what had to be done. Those parasites were costing your dad more than you will ever know."

He continued, "I know. But I was one of those parasites. Were they doing it because I was setting a bad example? Were they thinking if I could get away with it, why not they?"

She answered, "So what if they were thinking that way? They were still wrong. Why didn't one of them go to your dad and squeal on you? They didn't go because they were not his friends, and they wanted to protect their own little scam."

Then she went on to say, "Have you thought about the impact the news of those top executives getting fired is going to have on the hard-hats? Well, I will bet my bottom dollar, if there are any hard-hats shirking their duties, this move will make them see the light. I will bet the overall quality of work performance goes up."

Dalton thought a moment, then said, "Peg, I am finding more reasons to love you every day. You are right."

She said, "We are going to make a good team."
He answered, "I can't wait to get started."

Phase Two

THE NEXT MORNING Dalton dressed in a business suit and went to his dad's office.

His father greeted him with, "Are you ready for phase two?"

Dalton answered, "You bet I am. Let's start calling them in."

Of the 10 men and one woman who were dismissed, seven of their secretaries had literally been carrying them. The secretaries knew the business of the department in which they worked quite well, so there was no reason why they should not be offered the position first. Mr. Heinkle had already placed a call to one of the women. She arrived shortly after Dalton did. She was asked to come in and have a seat.

"Did Fred tell you about the meeting yesterday morning?"

She answered, "No, he didn't, But I am glad, with him not here, to have a chance to talk to you, because I simply cannot work for that man any more."

"Oh? And do you mind telling me why?"

She continued, "This might cost me my job, but if it does, so be it. He is not only a lecher; he is incompetent; he is lazy and he has me doing all his work."

Mr. Heinkle looked at Dalton. Dalton looked at his dad; then they both looked at Sara and back to each other.

Mr. Heinkle remarked, "How about that? Well, I'll tell you what, Sara. Fred got his ass canned in that meeting yesterday; that's the reason he never mentioned it. And the reason you are here is that I am aware you have been doing his work. So I am offering you his position, if you are interested."

She was totally thunderstruck.

Dalton asked her, "Well, Sara, how about it? Do you want the job?"

She answered, "Of course, I want the job!"

Mr. Heinkle said, "Your pay will not be the same as we were paying, or I should say giving, to Fred. We are reducing the pay of all central office executives. For instance, my annual salary has been $250,000, plus bonuses. Dalton will be taking over as president on January 1 for half that amount. Your annual salary will be $90,000 plus the same fringe benefits all employees will get.

She put the palms of her hands to the sides of her face and said, "Oh, my God! You two are not pulling my leg, are you?"

They both said, "No, we are not."

Dalton then said, "Okay, is it a deal?"

He extended his hand to her."

She said, as she shook his hand, "Oh, Lord, Please don't let me cry."

By the end of the meeting, four individuals had been replaced with the secretaries who were doing their work anyway. The fifth of the secretaries decided not to take the job. They eliminated three positions, including the one Dalton had been assigned; and they consolidated all the rest.

It was now time to talk to Henry about the chief engineer's job. Dalton walked down the stairs and into the boiler room. Henry was working at the workbench with something as Dalton entered.

Henry turned toward Dalton. He put one hand on his hip as he held a wrench in the other. "Well, I'll just be damned; Gabe was right; he told me he was sure he knew you from somewhere. I don't know who in the hell you are, but you are not Oscar. What is going on around here?"

"No, Henry, I am not who I was pretending to be. I am Dalton Heinkle, Jr. And my dad is retiring; I am taking over the business."

"I have heard about some of the changes that took place yesterday. Looks like you and the old man took my list to heart."

"Henry, we will never be able to repay you for the good you have brought about. Dad already knew a lot of what you told us, but your information confirmed it."

Henry turned back to the chore he was doing. "Are you making any other changes?"

"That's why I am down here. I am offering you the position of chief engineer."

Henry slowly placed the wrench he was holding on the bench. "You better not be bullshitting me, boy."

"I am not bullshitting you, Henry. The position is yours, if you want it."

Dalton extended his hand and Henry grasped it firmly. "When do I start?"

Henry accepted the position of chief engineer, and the man holding that position retired. They created one new position, director of children's services, and they planned to house that new division in the space vacated by the consolidations This reorganization of the executive offices would save the company at least $850,000 next year, not considering bonuses. Mr. Heinkle figured the mansion would bring two million dollars.

He said, "One of the guys at the country club has been hinting for me to sell the place to him ever since your mother passed away. I think I will let him have it for $3,000,000, provided he keeps Ruth and Sal on his staff. I am keeping the cook."

Dalton added, "Before you sell it, I want to take enough furniture from it to set up housekeeping in one of those bigger rentals."

When he walked into Millie's house that evening, the phone was ringing. He picked up the receiver and said, "Hello."

Peggy said, "Dalton, I can't allow any more time to pass being separated from you. I am loading all my belongings into a U-Haul, and I am coming home as soon as I can get there. You make another appointment with Judge Hemmingway. I've decided we don't need a big formal wedding."

Dalton thought, *"My God, I'm going to bawl again."*

Then he asked, "But what about your summer school obligation?"

She answered, "The whole staff voted on it. They decided, unanimously, they didn't need a 'cow-eyed' lovesick employee continually telling them about her perfect man any more."

THE END